Avatar of the Raven God

BRIAN PHILLIPS

DEDICATION

I dedicate this novella to my wife Laurie, who has always been a fan of the 'woman with a big sword' characters in fantasy novels. While she loves the power and violence that such figures may deliver, she is not such a fan of the 'tragic back story trope' so commonly tied to these characters. In this story, our main character Annah has no such baggage and swings a blade with the ferocity of a tiger and without any heartbreaking baggage.

OTHER BOOKS BY BRIAN PHILLIPS

LOST CITY

The wagon came to a halt in the empty market square. Dust hung in the air; the light brown haze settled around the rickety wooden thing. Its trail lagged, leaving a marker where it had moved across the sand-covered roads. The desert began to claim the city a hundred years ago. The ancient city continued to struggle against its fate. Someday the desert would swallow all of it. For today, the place continued to survive.

A tall guard walked to the wagon. He stood in the heat, fighting the worst of the sun by dressing in light tan robes head to toe. A thin, light cloth covered his face blocking the sun.

"Out!" The guard shouted as he removed the iron pin from the cage. The cage took up the entire bed of the wagon. Five people began to move. The cage wasn't tall enough to stand in. They crouched as each of them made their way through the door. One at a time, they climbed down onto the ground and stretched.

The last person in the cage came down. Tall and muscular, she stood out from the rest of the passengers, beauty mixed

1

with a warrior's strength to live in this woman's body. Her dark hair hung dirty and unwashed from the two-month journey to the city. A single thin scar ran down from her ear, crossing her throat at an angle, ending on her opposite shoulder. She scowled as she looked at the guard, assessing him and finding him unworthy.

"You're it? Are you supposed to keep us captive? Where's everyone else?" The woman put a hint of scorn into her voice as if she doubted that the guard could stop her, let alone all five of them.

The guard smiled back. "I told you. You aren't a captive. At least now that we are in the city. The wagon simply brings people here, it doesn't try to enslave them. Once we arrive, you are free to go and do as you wish."

The woman's face squinted back at him, confused. "Why did you haul us all the way out here then? You paid off the jailers to get five people into your cage, but you say that you aren't slavers?"

The guard looked back at her, taking his time, allowing his eyes to take in every one of her ample curves, her muscular arms, and her dazzling blue eyes. If it weren't for all the muscles and the scar across her neck, the guard thought she could have been the most beautiful woman in the city. She looked too dangerous to be anyone's trophy woman. That intrigued him. He wanted to reach out and touch her, to dare fate.

One of the male passengers walked past him toward the edge of the market square, tracking his movement. He seemed to be taking the guard at his word, claiming his freedom immediately.

"It's fine. I won't stop you. Go ahead." The guard called out to him before he returned his attention to the woman.

"Your name is Annah, right?"

"Obviously. Everyone's been calling me by that name the whole trip," Annah responded, scowling back at him.

"This is a tough place to make your way. I've made three trips here in the past year. Out of every load of people that I bring, one or two are dead by the time I return."

"I'll be careful," She replied, dismissively. She didn't feel under threat, at least now that she was out of the cage.

"I just wanted to let you know that I have a nice safe place to live here in the city. I could be useful for you, especially in your first days. I could make your life comfortable." The guard offered a lecherous grin before continuing, "If you made me comfortable. You know?"

A shiver of disgust ran down Annah's spine. She knew what he meant. Annah smiled back, offering an encouraging gaze.

"Oh, I know what you mean."

Her smile was filled with promise. The guard smiled back.

"All right!" The guard began. Then Annah's fist smashed into his nose. Blood sprayed out as his head snapped back. His eyes rolled up as he fell onto his knees. Blinking in surprise, the guard tried to speak.

"What?" He stammered.

It was the only word he could say before Annah's other fist slammed into his cheek. His head snapped to the right, and he collapsed onto the dirt. She took a single step back, then turned to look at him on the ground. She stepped forward and kicked him in the gut with her right leg. His body lifted off the ground and spun over, landing hard on his back.

"Stay clear of me, shite head. Next time I see you, I'll kill you." Annah knew the truth of that threat. She had no time for scum like this.

Annah turned around and walked toward the open streets. She motioned for the remaining three people to join her. They looked back and forth at each other, at the guard curled up on the ground, then at the open streets. They rushed to join her.

"Well done," a massive, blond-haired man with two months of wild beard growth said. He moved swiftly despite his large build, "My name's Eadgar," he said. Eadgar reached forward and offered her a companionable pat on the back.

Annah spun in place, confronting him. Her eyes narrowed. "Don't touch me."

Eadgar held his hands up, surprised at her reaction. He

offered an apology, "Sorry, I didn't mean to offend."

Looking at Eadgar, she evaluated how he stood, how he moved, and his facial expression that appeared genuinely surprised. Eadgar stood almost two hands taller than her. He looked like he had been bred for hard labor or war. Muscles the size of bread loaves stood out from his sun-scarred arms. Eadgar's voice held her attention, though. It sounded sincere, reverberating with both kindness and patience. She decided there were people more threatening in the world than Eadgar, and he might just end up being a useful ally in this strange place.

"Don't touch me again," Annah snapped back, then softened her approach as she saw his face change to concern, "at least not without asking first." She offered, trying to smile reassuringly back as she led the group into the city.

Trent and Cook, the two other travelers from the wagon, followed behind. Trent leaned over towards Cook's ear and spoke a few quiet words, "Some people have all the luck."

Cook waited for a few heartbeats before he responded, "That doesn't look like luck to me. I don't see an ounce of luck in this entire cursed town."

They wandered the streets for an hour. Eadgar wiped sweat from his forehead, then held up a hand indicating they should pause.

"This heat is killing me. Can I get a little rest in the shade?" Eadgar said.

"You've got to be kidding me. A big strong man like you can't take the heat?" Annah said, a playful mocking smile on her lips.

Eadgar frowned back at her. "If you are going to be a jerk, I'll just go find my own place to rest."

"Don't be like that," Annah said, "I'm only teasing."

"I'm with Eadgar. It's hot and we aren't doing anything but wandering around hoping to find a deserted building that might be livable," Cook said, "all of these buildings are abandoned, and they are all just about ready to collapse. I do not want to take shelter in anything we found so far. Let's grab some shade and take a rest. I vote we wait for it to cool off, then head to the center of this place and look for a building that has been repaired. Maybe we can find one that isn't under threat of falling on our heads."

Trent laughed out loud, "There you go with that thinking again," then he pointed farther along the road. A building stood at the end of the street, unremarkable except that someone had arranged some old dead trees from the second story window, then draped a long cloth over it the brittle branches. The shadow cast along the street was large enough so they could all fit within it.

"How about there?" Trent asked.

"Sure, I'll take just about anything right now."

They turned and walked down the street. A few minutes later, Eadgar walked beneath the cloth awning and took up a position against the building. He slid down the wall until he was seated on the hard-packed dirt that made up the street. Trent followed closely behind, then Cook. Annah stood in the sunlight for a few more seconds, staring down at them as if in judgment, then joined the group in the shade. The others had filled the available wall, so Annah sat alone in the center of the shade.

She felt the others looking at her, trying to discover something. They didn't feel like a threat, but she had the feeling that some questions were coming.

"Better?" Annah asked, hoping to control the impending conversation.

"I think so," said Eadgar. Trent grunted in agreement.

A few moments passed in awkward silence. The city felt dead, no sounds came from the streets. There were no barking dogs, nor even footsteps. There was nothing. Moments stretched on to minutes, then became a score of minutes. Each minute felt the same as the last. She didn't like it. This place felt not only dead but dare she say, boring.

Eadgar began to speak. Somehow that didn't surprise her. Eagar was the most outgoing of the four of them.

"We spent a few weeks in that cage," he began, "During that little trip, I discovered a lot about everyone. Trent was arrested by the guard for thievery. He bribed the guards to let him go, so the guards sold him to the caravan."

Trent nodded as his eyes cracked open. "Not the best plan, but it kept me from getting my hand chopped off. I didn't know about the cage though, that just sort of happened."

Eadgar continued, "And Cook was, well, a cook. He got in a fight with someone influential and got sent off to the caravan to avoid further problems."

Cook just nodded, grimacing at the ordeal remaining silent about the details of his capture. He had spoken at length while they were in the cage. There had been plenty of time for stories back then and Cook knew how to tell one.

"But you, Annah, you didn't tell us much about how you got to the cage," Eadgar said.

"I told you what you needed to know," Annah replied coldly.

Eagar nodded thoughtfully, not as if he were agreeing with Annah, but as if he were slowly processing what she said, making sure he understood all of its layered meaning.

Eadgar began speaking again, "That was back in the cage. Right now, all four of us are depending on each other. We need to know the details. Did you murder someone? Are you an arsonist? We need to decide if we can count on each other here. So far, I don't have much information that creates trust in you."

Annah gazed back into Eadgar's eyes, then moved her gaze to pass over Trent's, then Cook. All three stared back expectantly. A minute passed in silence before Annah let out a defeated breath.

"Alright, here it is," she began reluctantly, "I got captured during a battle."

Eadgar's face turned white as the obvious consequences to a woman captured in battle dawned on him, "I am so sorry."

Annah held up her palm to stop him, "Save your sorrow, it wasn't like that. I was part of a foot company that had been left to guard a road against bandits. We got raided by about a hundred horsemen, and there were only ten of us."

She tried to end the story there, but the others looked on expectantly. After another moment of silence, she turned her head and spit in disgust before returning to her story.

"We never even drew our blades. Those bandits had been raiding our lands for weeks, killing and looting. We never even drew steel, we just surrendered like meek little kittens."

Trent asked the first question, "Wait, you were a ground troop? As a woman?"

Annah cracked a smirk, "Yes, I was a swordswoman. I know it is unusual in some places, but in my home country, it is common. I'm not sure of the history, but a few centuries ago the ruling family decided that they needed everyone strong enough to fight to be in the army. I think it saved the country from some army or another. Since then about a third of the army has been women, and we've never lost a war."

"What? That's it? You joined the army because that's people normally do? Don't you have a tragic story of loss and revenge?" Trent asked.

"Not for me, there's been plenty of loss and death, but somehow my family avoided it. Like I told you, my people get raided a lot. Men and women are killed and robbed every year. When I was younger, I decided that I wanted to fight as my father and cousin had done, so I joined the army. Since then it's been a lot of traveling, guarding, ambushing, and on a good day, fighting."

"Fighting on a good day?" Eadgar asked.

"Sure. Someone needs to put things right. A little more justice in the world is a good thing, and if I'm the one who administers it, so much the better."

"You like killing?" Trent asked.

"No," Annah replied, "I like the feeling when I realize that I just saved someone's life, someone's farm, someone's family. It is just that easy. There is evil in the world and someone needs to kill it.

Another uncomfortable silence descended on the group. They sat on the hard-baked mud of the street watching the afternoon sun move slowly towards the horizon.

Eadgar interrupted the silence, "You missed your era."

"What?" Annah replied, confused.

Eadgar said, "A few centuries ago, people would have said that you were touched by the gods. They would have given you gifts of food and wine to entice you to visit their towns, and perhaps right whatever wrongs you found there."

"And you know this because?" Annah asked.

"Because my grandfather told me. He was the last shaman we had in our village. My people worshiped the Turtle God for centuries. After the Turtle God stopped coming to the village, we kept on in our ways. We kept our old customs for three generations of shamans. He told me a lot."

"So, are you the new shaman then?" Cook asked, interest evident in his voice.

"No, my grandfather was the last. When he passed through the final door, he didn't bother naming the next shaman to follow him. His last words were that the gods were gone. He told me not to bother with the old ways."

Annah said, "I don't follow those ways. I just follow my sword, and my sword tells me that the sun is low enough for us to resume our search."

The four of them began to stand, then stretch out their muscles. Cook brushed the sand from his clothing, creating a cloud of dust that hung languidly in the air before it descended back to the earth. They turned their backs on the building and walked toward the city center.

TREASURE HUNT

The next morning brought pain. The unmerciful sun shone down on Annah's skin. There had only been three hours since sunrise, and already her skin had begun to cook.

Their previous night's search for a safe place to sleep had been a failure.

"Oh, shite." She cursed as she rolled over. Sand covered the left side of her face where she had laid for the night. The sun bore into her eyes with unrelenting fury. Rubbing her eyes and wiping the sand away, she looked at the dying city around her.

"You said it." Eadgar groused as he crawled into conscious. The four of them, all unfortunate passengers of the cage, began to awaken. The previous night came into clarity. Inns and boarding houses filled the city, but none of them were charities. The people who lived in this city thought it was normal to be captured in other places, then released onto the streets. They had met five other people that arrived here in the same unfortunate way.

Luckily, Annah thought, the weather held last night, and

sleeping in the street wasn't unusual even among the city dwellers. No one had disturbed them. She didn't believe the ordinary citizen of this city was necessarily honest, more like they simply looked too poor to bother with robbing.

A shadow passed between Annah and the bright sun. She looked up to see who blocked the light. A man stood over her. He wasn't tall for a man, only a half-hand shorter than her. He looked well-groomed, dressed like a merchant with lightweight silks died the color of night. Calf-high boots may have looked elegant only a few years ago, now they stood coated with the cities dust, their leather soles cracked.

"Welcome to our city, strangers," The man said, while he grinned down at her. It wasn't a lecherous grin. Instead, it seemed to delight at an inside joke.

"Bugger off." Her first instinct told her to react violently to this brazen stranger. Annah wanted to avoid trouble with the locals, but she wasn't going to tolerate any of their nonsense either.

Eadgar sat up, rubbing his eyes for a moment, trying to recover his vision in the face of the sun's harsh glare. "Hold on, let's be friends here." He said as he struggled up, trying to push off the sleep that wanted to hold him in its grasp. Eadgar held his hand out, welcoming the stranger in the way his people did. The stranger didn't seem to understand the greeting. Instead, he took Eadgar's hand in his and pulled him up, assisting him off the ground.

"You make friends quickly," Cook said as he got to his feet. The hard journey in the wagon had not been kind to Cook, and the cold night's sleep hadn't helped him either.

Cook scratched his short gray beard while Eadgar began to laugh. "I can't help it. I'm just a friendly person." Eadgar said. He looked down at the stranger's hand, still in his grasp. He finally shook it in greeting, as was the habit of northerners. Eadgar towered over the stranger, standing a head taller and outweighing him by at least five stone. "My name is Eadgar, well met. This is Cook, Trent is our friend pretending to be asleep over there," Eadgar pointed at Trent's prone body, "and this is Annah. Don't let her beauty fool you, she's a tiger."

"A tiger, is she? I like tigers." The stranger shook Eadgar's hand in a tight grip, apparently aware of the custom after all. "My name is Easter. I'm a foreigner here as well. I didn't come the usual way what with the wagons and all, but I'm here now, trying to make my fortune."

"Where is here?" Annah asked as she gazed left and right, taking in the decrepit brown building that populated this dying city, a hint of annoyance in her voice.

"Oh, no one told you? This dying city was once known as Tascarcoda. This city is so old we think it was built before the gods were born. Now we just call it the Desert City since it is the only city out here in the middle of this wasteland."

"Really? Before the Horse God?" Eadgar asked, skepticism dripping from his voice.

Trent rolled his eyes, used to Eadgar's fascination with the gods. Cook tried to stay away from such things.

"Oh no," Easter disagreed, "obviously not before the First Gods. They were first, after all. I meant before men found a way to become gods."

Cook replied with skepticism, "So this place doesn't have a god?"

"No. This place is dripping with old ways, old magic, and old secrets. Once you've been here a while, I'm sure you will become fascinated with this place. The gods are different here, like everywhere, but here is special. This place has two gods."

"Two?" Cook asked with a hint of fear in his voice.

"Yes, we have Water Mother, a kind and benevolent goddess who has a temple in the center of the city. Go there if you need help with cuts, bruises, or disease. Her followers will always help, well normally anyway. Sometimes they ask for donations and all that..."

"And the other?" Trent asked.

"That would be Father Desert, lord of heat, sand, bugs, and all the things you are going to hate about this place," Easter said.

"What about his temple?" Trent said, trying to find out more about this mysterious Father Desert.

Easter waved back and forth in front of him, indicating a vast expanse of view, "He lives out in the desert somewhere, of course. Father Desert seldom comes to the city. I think he enjoys the company of scorpions more than men. The city is interesting, but the ruins out in the desert, fascinating."

Annah frowned. "I'm fascinated with battles, that doesn't mean I want to stay in one."

"Well said. This place is special. I have never found a place that supplied such a quick way to make a fortune. This city is overflowing with treasures, at least if you are brave enough to look for them."

"Treasures?" Trent asked, abandoning his concern with the gods.

Easter turned toward him, inclining his head. "Yes, treasures. This city is old, underpopulated, and in its death throes. Many people come here in the hopes of discovering a magical artifact. Magicians give rewards for such things. In some cases, the finder simply keeps what they discover, making its power their own."

"Wait a minute," Eadgar began, "if it is so easy to discover these artifacts, why isn't this place overflowing with people?"

Easter offered a smile before he began his explanation. "It used to be less difficult than it is now. The easily reached treasures have mostly been found. Only the challenging ones remain. Traps, curses, and even monsters may block the path of treasure seekers. These magical artifacts seem to pull danger toward them. Not everyone can find an artifact. Well, to be honest, most people give up early in their search, or perish in the process."

"Is that what brought you here? Searching for artifacts?" Eadgar asked.

"Or just picking over the dead?" Annah added, a hint of skepticism in her voice.

"Mostly both. I'm part of a larger group of people who came here to collect these artifacts. That task has proved more challenging than we originally anticipated. Right now, we focus on helping newcomers get started, and we purchase these artifacts whenever people bring them to us."

"There's the hook," Annah said, annoyance dripping from her voice, "You and your friends encourage newcomers to go get themselves killed so you can get some trinkets. Let me guess, we bring you a magic thingy, you steal it. No, thanks."

"Hardly," Easter responded with a laugh. "We have been here for more than a decade and intend to be here much longer. Our pockets are deep enough that many newcomers have come, stayed a successful year or two, then left to return home rich beyond their wildest dreams."

Cook snorted. "What about the unsuccessful ones?"

Easter shook his head. "Some are still here, seeking their fortune. Some, well, aren't." Easter didn't need to say what happened to those that were no longer here. They wouldn't be collecting artifacts for anyone.

"What about if we just left? We could catch the next wagon north and just leave," Annah said.

"You could do that. Caravans come and go about every month or two, depending on the season. No one is going to stop you."

A moment passed as the group looked around the street where they had awoken. Dust moved through the street in clouds, stinging as it touched their skin. The sun beat down relentlessly, bringing thirst and fatigue. Annah thought about the month-long wagon ride that had brought them here, about the water they had consumed, about the wastelands they had passed, about the cage.

"How much does a caravan out of this place normally cost, if I could be so bold to ask?" Annah said.

Easter pursed his lips, as if in concentration. Annah wasn't fooled, he had come prepared for this exact conversation.

"Caravan rides out of here generally cost a hundred silver

coins, more if you want the luxury treatment."

Cook took in a quick intake of breath. A hundred silver coins could pay a prince's ransom. For a month's passage, it was unthinkable.

Trent laughed, his crisp bark echoing from the abandoned buildings lining the street. "A hundred silver? It seems a bit excessive."

"I agree," Easter said, "but there are taxes and such. The city guild charges thirty silver coin fee to those who don't hunt treasures, it's their way to motivate more explorers to stay. Also, Father desert takes his thirty coins as well, leaving forty to hire a few wagons, supply them with food and water, and then a few guards."

"Guards in the desert? Who's going to attack us out there?" Eadgar asked, confused.

Easter offered a sympathetic grin, "Scorpions, the desert is full of them."

"Scorpions? Do we need guards for insects? Seriously?"

"The scorpions are the size of horses. Did you forget where we were? Even with the four of you, you'll need a few more competent swords available if you want to reach your destination alive."

"And the only way that we can afford to raise that kind of silver is to dig through these old ruins, am I right?" Annah said, a sarcastic note in her voice, "how did I ever guess that little trick?"

"No need to guess, I'll confirm it. If you want to leave, find a little treasure, and get out of here. You might find it easier than you expect. Truthfully, I find hunting through these ruins exiting." Easter replied.

"Again, I find battles exciting, that doesn't mean I want to hunt for them."

Trent spoke before Annah could reply, "Let's assume that we four want to risk our meager lives in search of these treasures. Can you tell us where even to start?"

"Sure, I can do that," Easter said, confident he had set the hook.

OFFICIAL BUSINESS

Master Easter looked up at the stone keep towering above him. The keep's shadow covered him in blessed darkness, shielding his skin from the harsh sun for just a few cherished moments. He thought about the trials that awaited him within. His old master, Master Mooterah, may have returned from his desert exploration by now.

Easter hoped not. He despised Mooterah with all his heart. Every month Easter made a secret curse in his heart for Master Mooterah. Easter cursed him to be devoured by the desert, cursed him to be lost and never found. Mooterah had achieved his master's ring a hundred years ago. There was little chance of him traveling through the final black door, at least not of him staying there. Easter's curses were weak things in any case; only wishes of the heart and not spells cast into the world.

He walked toward the tower's door. Two solid oak doors stood in front of him, each twice his height. A round door knocker recently forged of iron stood out from each of their surfaces, waiting to be pulled. Scars decorated the wood where old fixtures had been removed, each injury holding the animal outline of a First God.

The totem door handles were gone now. Easter wished that the First Gods would follow those handles as they left this world. He shivered as he reached out for the door ring. Ten years ago, long before he achieved his own master's ring, these door handles had been in the shape of ravens. Easter remembered how the old door rings would glint in the sunlight, even though they were composed of complete black metal. The door rings had been shaped like ravens, flying in a circle, decorated each handle. This building had been a temple to one of the First Gods less than fifty years ago. It served the Raven God, the incarnation of justice, predator, carrion-eater, vengeance server. The First Gods seem to have left the world, but not completely. Their mark remained throughout the city, everywhere Easter looked.

Easter pulled the door open to reveal a dim corridor. He walked forward, allowing the dim light to guide his way. A single form stood guard at the entrance dressed head to foot in chain mail. Once the guard was a man, now it had become more than a man. The thing stood quietly, enchanted with the strength of a mountain and the will of a flea. The sentry's armored form stood entirely still, not bothering to challenge Easter, his black master's ring evidence enough to his right to pass.

One couldn't counterfeit a master's ring after all. The rings were made of souls. If anyone could do such a thing, then they must be a master necromancer as well.

A necromancer must sacrifice part of themselves to craft a ring. Plenty of people had tried sacrificing the souls of others, and it had never worked. Only monsters could be created in that way, and not the kind easily controlled.

Easter walked past without a word. He shook his head as he passed, knowing that socializing with the sentry was as useless as socializing the door itself. Someday, the thought, he should investigate how to restore these men and women who had been changed into sentries. Their souls had not been taken entirely from them. There might be shreds of it left somewhere in there. Perhaps, he thought, someday they might be healed.

A dark wooden staircase stood against the right wall, rising from the floor at a gentle angle. The tower stood fifty paces across, tall for any structure so old. It had been particularly unusual with its detailed construction, ornate stonework, and devout woodcarvings.

Those woodcarvings had been removed years ago, at the command of Master Mooterah. The once-ornate stair posts now stood plain, shorn of their previous carvings and artwork. At one point just a few years ago, there was no buttress, no rafter, no beam that did not have a First God carved onto its surface. The Ram God had guarded over the stairs, the Horse God had looked on from the walls, and ever-vigilant Raven God had been everywhere, looking on in stern disapproval.

They were all gone now. Easter wondered how long they would remain away.

He continued up the stairs, ignoring the slight shiver that passed up his spine. He didn't know what had gotten his guard up. So far, he reflected, it had been a useful day. Two more explorer parties had returned with a few valuable artifacts. None of which helped inform him as to the history of Tascarcoda, but that didn't surprise him. He turned onto the second floor. An apprentice sat on a chair behind a large, yet plainly decorated wooden desk. Small cracks had started to form in the desk's surface, testifying to the dry weather's power over mere wood.

"Good day Gustavo, any news?" Easter asked the apprentice.

The apprentice stood, albeit slower than he might for a more senior master. This apprentice remembered when Easter had been alongside him a mere five years ago and had yet to be either impressed or terrified. Easter offered a friendly smile, and the apprentice finally responded.

"Just the usual, Water Mother sends word that she needs supplies and offers food in return. Six fights broke out in some inns."

"Fights? How is this news?" Easter asked.

"Three of them involved apprentices. My partner Tegan got sent to the Water Mother with a broken nose."

"Ah," Easter replied with a hint of a laugh, "and do the brave apprentices plan to go forth in battle and exact vengeance?"

"Maybe, we haven't decided yet. Sometimes it's worth the trouble, sometimes it isn't." The apprentice replied.

Easter walked up and stood directly across from the young man, gazing at him from shoes to hair for a moment, then meeting his eyes, showing a hint of his master's power. "Don't do anything stupid. Keep in mind that if you interrupt the search effort, your master will be disappointed in you. One of the first real lessons you need to learn as a necromancer is that your ego means nothing, and it can only get you killed, or in this game, worse than killed. Save that stupidity for when you gain your ring."

The apprentice nodded, a frown appearing on his face as if Easter had discovered some deep secret he had tried to hideaway. Easter stepped back and offered a sympathetic smile. "Good. I'll be going upstairs for a few hours. Admit anyone who calls on me, I'm open for business."

"Are you expecting someone, Master Easter?" The apprentice said, adding the formality at the end.

"Just a few more explorers who arrived yesterday. My intuition tells me they might be particularly useful."

Nodding, the apprentice sat back down in his chair. He had learned years ago not to doubt Easter's intuition.

Turning from the apprentice, Easter walked up to another set of wooden stairs. These stairs had been equally stripped of its carvings and designs. He had to admit that he preferred the building as they initially found it, alive with images of First Gods, and decorated with symbols of their worship.

Even if the First Gods cared nothing for the ways of men, the carvings had created an aura of life in this tower. Now that the figures had been removed and the necromancer masters installed, it felt more like a mausoleum than a temple.

He arrived on the third floor. A set of stairs continued up the tower along the adjoining wall. An empty desk stood in front of a bare flat wall; sections recently carved clean of their artwork. Three doors stood against the wall. Easter looked at the empty desk where apprentice Tegan should be. He shook his head in amusement, then walked to the other side of it. He reached down and touched a journal that had been left behind. Easter opened it and glanced at its content. Tables of numbers filled the book, each entry listed beside the description of a found item, the weight, the reward paid, and the finder's name.

After confirming that it was Tegan's handwriting in the book, Easter concentrated a moment, opening his spirit channels to find the ghost-like imprint of Apprentice Tegan. A small hint, like a feather's touch, stroked across Easter's channeling. He nodded. He felt confident this book would do its job in his next spell. Shifting his spirit channels, he formed a channeled knot, then impressed a vision of Tegan from his memory. He released the knot and felt his channel expand as the knot hunted for its prey.

By the time Easter felt the channel surge, confirming its mission, he had already entered the third door and sat at his own desk. His room stood nearly empty, only three boxes rested on the floor, recently emptied of useless trinkets found by the explorers. Easter reached out to follow the spirit trail left by his crafting. He felt the usual disorientation as his perceptions left his body and sped through the dying city of Tascarcoda. Moments later, his vision slowed. Easter looked down on Tegan as he lay upon a stone bench, a series of cushions beneath him.

The most beautiful woman Easter had ever seen sat at the foot of the bench. Easter opened his channels further, bringing the remote scene in, closer to his conscious soul.

"Let that be a lesson then," Phyllis said to Tegan, "picking fights with people who fight professionally isn't the best plan for an apprentice magician."

"Necromancer." Tegan corrected a hint of scorn in his voice.

"Of course," Phyllis apologized, "I'm not familiar with how you differentiate yourselves from other magicians. I'll try to use that word from now on."

"You're having me on," Tegan said, "I just told you that last week. You're way smarter than that."

She smiled back.

"And you're getting beat up in town to get a free trip to the Water Temple. Is it just to see me, or have you developed an interest in serving the Water Mother?"

Easter watched from his spectral place as Tegan leered at Phyllis, his eyes resting on her ample form. He knew that he shouldn't interrupt, but the Order had a reputation to consider, and being churlish to the people that provided the water in the middle of the desert didn't seem like a good idea to him.

Easter opened his channels a bit further, exposing his presence to both Tegan and Phyllis. A black aura emerged next to them, showing an image of Easter. "Tegan, if you are quite done, then return. Your work eagerly awaits you."

Tegan looked back at Easter's form. He had seen this trick before.

"It isn't busy. I'll be back in plenty of time." Tegan said, trying to gain more time with the lovely Phyllis.

"Either you get back here right now, or I send you out with the next search party. It's your pick."

Tegan frowned, remembering two other apprentices that had never returned from such adventures.

EASTER'S MASTER

His footsteps sounded like they moved inside of a drum as Easter paced within his office sanctuary. The nearly empty room echoed with the sounds of his wooden-soled boots marching across the smooth polished wooden floor. Nothing was out of place, everything was carefully minimized, all clutter removed.

He didn't trust it. He had initially kept the room spotless to ensure that any hidden visitors would have a difficult time staying quiet. The unintended consequence of that decision was that he had made it easier for Master Mooterah to visit him unannounced.

Now Easter had the feeling that his old master watched him from some invisible perch. He thought about opening his magic channels, but every time he dispelled Mooterah's craftings, Mooterah took affront. An affronted necromancer wasn't a good thing, especially when they needed to cooperate over the next decade or so, or at least until this city was wholly scoured

23

of magical items.

As if Easter's thoughts summoned him, Mooterah slowly faded into the room as if he had come from thin air. His tall form, almost two hands taller than Easter, stood ridiculously high as he floated a foot from the floor. Master Mooterah had long ago mastered the art of hiding spells, and he had recently added levitation in an ego-fueled effort to avoid Easter's notice. Mooterah seemed to enjoy skulking in shadows and surprising the unwary.

That was a useful skill, Easter had to admit to himself. A necromancer could always benefit from judicious hiding when necessary. Mooterah seemed to be taking the talent to a whole new level.

Now Mooterah stood in his office. Easter offered a slight bow of respect to his former master and walked to his chair, putting the desk between them.

"I haven't seen you for a few days." Easter began.

Mooterah's voice came out rough as if it were made of the same sand the desert had formed from. "Did you miss me?" Mooterah asked, his voice dripping with sarcasm.

Easter offered a slight grin. He had missed Mooterah's presence as much as he had missed any cancer. If the conclave hadn't given him a direct command to work alongside Mooterah, Easter would have never done it. Serving the man had been bad enough, and the ordeal he had passed through to gain his master's ring had been horrifying. Mooterah did love the horror in things.

Easter spoke softly with each word wrapped in a veil of threat, "Let's not dwell on our feelings, at least not at this moment." There would be time enough for that. Easter's feelings involved sliding a dagger through Mooterah's eye, piercing his brain, and leaving him in the desert to rot. Sadly, he thought it was unfortunate that Masters of the White Hand wouldn't stay beyond the final black door of death permanently. Mooterah certainly deserved a long absence from the world in any case.

"Did you find anything useful?" Easter asked, trying to regain some semblance of a conversation.

"I found clues, not much else. The map led me to an old tower. It hadn't been searched yet. Sadly, only the bodies remained. Like always, I tried to pull back their souls and interrogate them. That same force blocked me."

Nodding, Easter motioned him to continue. Some force of magic had been interfering with their necromancy since they had arrived in this city. No one had discovered its source, at least not yet.

"The tower stands two weeks from the city. There is no imaginable way that something in the city is the problem. It's got to be more than an enchantment."

"Back to that argument again, ey? Do you think the First Gods would bother with this place? Look around. It's dying."

"Exactly," Mooterah spit out, "and the entire White Hand Order can't stop it. We've slowed its rate of decay, but we don't seem to be able to restore the city. It holds its secrets jealously, intent on bringing them along to the grave with it. Spells don't do that. I'm telling you; this city is cursed by the First Gods. The desert encroaches further every year. The winds grow stronger, and living things grow more barren. We can barely grow food now, and as you know, if it were not for the Water Mother, we would have no food or water at all."

"Have you found any hint of the First Gods then? Have you seen their presence?"

"It doesn't work like that," Mooterah said, "not all of the First Gods act directly. We may not be dealing with something like the Wolf God and his packs. We might be enmeshed with something more sinister."

That got Easter's attention. "More sinister than a ravenous First God that converts his followers into berserkers?"

Mooterah shook his head, unhappy with his lack of evidence. He dearly wanted to save this city, to scrub it clean of its magical secrets. The desert, the wind, and fate itself seemed against him.

"But I've got one more place to look," Mooterah said.

"Really? Look for what?" Easter replied.

"Look for the First Gods. I found a prayer stone in the last tower I visited. It mentioned that one of the First Gods had liked to dwell near the graves, among cairn stones not far from that tower I had recently discovered. I sent out some scouts. They found a set of burial cairns a few days from the tower. I'm going to resupply and head out again. Hopefully, our answers will be there in those abandoned graves. Want to come along and share the glory?"

Easter wasn't about to take his bait. "No, it's your glory. I'll stay here like a good secretary and keep the ledgers."

"Very well," Mooterah said, "don't let the cabal say I didn't offer to share." He turned and opened the door, pausing at the door he gave Easter a final message. "And don't let me find you out there without my direct permission. Keep to your place."

Easter bowed his head in submission. Mooterah walked from the room as Easter fantasized about Mooterah finding a First God alone in a graveyard.

Easter prayed in his secret heart that Mooterah would find such a thing and that First God would destroy his old master. Few people deserved it more.

GETTING READY

A group of fifty people filled the public square, which only last night had stood deserted. Annah stood watching the crowd of assembling treasure hunters in the early morning light. The caravan began to form up before dawn, and now small groups of people jostled with each other to claim a space in the line of men. Most traveled on foot with only four mules and a sun-worn cart to carry heavy loads. The successful treasure hunters guarded their valuable transport with jealous eyes, daring anyone to take advantage of them.

Annah glanced toward the rest of her small group. Cook stood next to her, quietly devouring the remains of whatever bird they had eaten and not finished last night. She shook her head in disgust. The bird had tasted like a combination of chicken and rotting fish then. She tried to imagine how disgusting it would taste this morning after a long night in Cook's pocket. Cook didn't seem to care.

Eadgar smiled over at her. She wondered for the twentieth time whether he was interested in her romantically, or if he was just that friendly of a person. In her experience, genuine friendliness tended to be rare. Eadgar seemed to have a positive outlook on everything as if every day was a new treat to be savored. She hoped that he would be the exception to the rule.

Trent glanced up from where he knelt, busily digging through bags of gear. Torches, rope, iron spikes, and a sack of dried fruit lay scattered about the packed dirt. Sand blew across their eight water flasks, sticking to a few small spilled droplets that struggled to survive the morning sun. They had begun with only one water flask for each of them until the caravan master had sent them back for more. The desert could forgive many things, but never a lack of water.

"It's amazing," Eadgar said, looking on in wonder.

"It's amazingly early," Annah said, "I'm still exhausted from last night. We need to find a better place to sleep."

"True, but when we get back from this little trip, we will be overflowing with treasure!" Eadgar said.

"Or overflowing in blood," Cook added.

Looking back and forth, Annah sighed. She felt disappointed in the caravan's lack of organization. She doubted that trekking into the desert with no plan would result in the piles of treasure Eadgar hoped for. She glanced around the crowd, noting how heavily-armed the crowd seemed to be, and how lightly armed their group was. Conditions could rapidly deteriorate out there, and not only the weather could turn against them.

"I don't see an empty wagon. It looks like we are carrying our gear on our backs." Annah said, resigned to an aching back at the end of the day.

"How about those mules?" Trent pointed out, gesturing toward two mules that wandered about the crowd untethered. Annah wondered why they were not tied in place, then she remembered how rare food would be for these animals. It seemed a miracle that any mules would be available at all.

"Those mules are owned by another group," Eadgar began to explain, "I spoke with some other treasure hunters last night in the tavern. There aren't many rules to this effort, but keeping your hands-off other people's mules, wagons, and tools is definitely one of them."

"We don't share?" Trent seemed surprised, now keenly aware of the small amount of gear he had available for their enterprise.

"No, sharing isn't a common trait among these treasure hunter groups. They don't even share plans. Most of the time, the caravan just wanders down a set path. Groups of us will leave the caravan when a promising trail intersects with the road. Ideally, the groups separate one at a time, so they don't get in each other's way."

Annah nodded, agreeing with the tactic. "Makes sense to me. No one wants treasure hunters fighting over spoils in the desert, I don't at least. How about water? The skins won't last a single day in this heat."

"The road will have wells alongside, dug at different intervals. Water won't be a problem until we separate." Eadgar explained.

Filling the last of his bags with gear, Trent hefted the final bag over his shoulder and stood up. It looked bulky and a little unwieldy, no different than many of the other treasure hunters. "Everyone grab a bag. Let's check in with the caravan master before it gets too hot." Trent said.

Pulling up a pair of water skins, Annah led the group into the mass of treasure hunters. She felt someone touch her elbow and puller her arm, capturing her attention. She turned her head, preparing an angry scowl for whoever had put hands on her and found Eadgar pointing into the crowd.

"Look, there's Easter. I guess we aren't the only group of people he recruited." Eadgar said.

"Odd, what is he up to?" Annah asked, watching him in the center of a group of six treasure hunters. They seemed to be in a conversation, leaning in to hear Easter's words. He didn't want to share anything with the crowd.

"Let's go insert ourselves and find out what's going on," Trent suggested, eager to get started with their journey.

"Maybe not. We don't need to come off as overly snoopy or

distrustful, at least not yet." Annah said as she shook her head, painfully aware of how little her single eating knife would protect her from the group of men surrounding Easter.

"Don't worry. I've got this." Trent said as he scampered off, separating from their group and joining the crowd. She watched as Trent moved deftly between the people in the crowd and arrived within arm's reach of Easter's group.

"What is he doing?" Eadgar asked, a laugh struggling to escape his chest, "He's a cheeky rouge, isn't he?"

A smile cracked Annah's facade. She had to grin at the sheer gutsiness of it. Viewed from the outside, it looked pretty evident that Trent was spying on the group. She had no doubt Easter would spot him as well. Annah wondered if it would cause problems, then considered the dying city around them. She doubted that those problems wouldn't be as bad as getting kidnapped and brought here in the first place.

"Do you see those people that just joined the crowd?" Eadgar asked. She hadn't, she had been paying exclusive attention to Trent's antics.

"No. What's the big deal?" She turned to look at the newcomers.

"I met them at the inn last night. The large one, their leader, complained that they had no weapons. Now every one of them is armed. Somehow they found a half-dozen blades overnight."

That gained Annah's attention. "Don't just stand here, go find out where they got the blades. My kitchen knife isn't going to do much out there if the Easter's tales of horse-sized scorpions prove to be true."

Eadgar walked toward the new group. Annah turned her attention back to Easter and his secret meeting.

The group had dispersed while she was distracted. She spotted Trent moving back their way, walking through the crowd, stopping to chat with people now and again. When Trent wasn't with people he had been imprisoned in a cage with, he seemed a lot friendlier. Of course, he also liked to spy on people.

She spotted Trent looking her way and waver her hand at him, motioning him to come back. He said a few words to finish his conversation, then walked up to her.

"Well?" Annah asked.

"I overheard Easter giving that group some direction. He says that the site they wanted to explore got cleaned out by someone who wasn't in the caravan. He told them to skip where they planned to search and wait for better pickings."

Her brow wrinkled as she thought about it. "I wonder how Easter finds out about these things."

"No idea. Easter did seem confident. He said that there were some unsafe ruins around their original site, and they should avoid that area at all costs." Trent said.

She lost interest when she saw Eadgar waving at her.

"I'll be right back." She said, leaving Trent and walking toward Eadgar.

"There's a pile of swords and stuff for anyone. They don't even charge money for them. I guess people find them in these ruins and just contribute them to a common pile. Do you want to pick one up before we go?"

"Yes," Annah said, relieved that something had finally gone their way. "But why are they being given away? Are they any good?"

"I guess finding weapons in ruins is a pretty common thing. Let's get some blades before the caravan leaves us behind. Follow me."

Jogging out of the square, Eadgar led her behind a building to an abandoned stable. One of the wooden walls had recently fallen, allowing easy access to the abandoned barn. She looked in and saw a long table that held a dozen swords, a mace, a few long knives, and a spear taller than a man.

"I can just take one?" She asked, unimpressed with the quality of the weapons on display.

"I guess so. I will need to supply a replacement in any case. If we find something out there, we can just return what we pick. If we find something worse, then we just contribute that back to the pile."

"Sounds like it is set up to collect poor quality weapons." She said unconvinced.

"Yes, poor quality equals free around here. Do you want one or not?" Eadgar asked.

Reaching out, she picked up a sword. It had a hint of rust along its edge. She grabbed the blade in one hand and tried to bend it. It held its shape.

"I can sharpen this one."

"Great." Eadgar reached out and picked up the spear, hefting it to test its weight. Then he picked up two other swords and tucked them into his belt.

"I've got enough for all of us."

"Who gets the spear?" Annah asked, surprised he would bother with such a thing. Spears were for use against horsemen, not for exploring ruins.

"Me, of course." He smiled as he hefted it, showing off its dark metal tip. Then he offered her a smile. "I've got a good feeling about this one."

GETTING TO KNOW YOU

The caravan of treasure hunters stretched back along the sand-covered track. Rolling dunes the size of castle walls blocked their way to the east. A single well stood in contrast to the bleak terrain. The well stood covered by a small wooden roof with no walls, only blocking the sun from the stone-reinforced hole in the earth. A single bucket lay next to the hole, rope connecting it to an iron spike jutting from the sand.

Eadgar looked on with suspicion. They had passed five wells over the three days of their journey. Only two of them had held water. Their group only had half of the water they started with, and it was only the third day. When he began this journey, he thought their biggest challenge was facing the creatures and traps in the ruins. He shook his head at his naivete. The biggest problem seemed to be surviving the desert. He would be thankful for a chance to fight back against the things trying to kill him.

Out here, the sun was trying to kill him. He didn't know how to fight back against the sun.

"Three coins on a dry well." Trent prodded him. He had started making bets yesterday, confident that more wells would be dry than not.

Cook spoke up. "You don't have three coins to rub together. I'm not playing your games. There's a lot more at stake than a few coins. If we don't have water, we'll have to turn back."

"What are you talking about? I'm six coins ahead since yesterday. Apparently, the last dry well had been full last month, and someone was feeling sure of themselves."

Before Cook could admonish him for his perpetual greed, Annah interrupted him.

"I'll take that bet." Annah said, her voice cutting through their banter, "I've got a feeling about this one."

The group gathered together to watch Wyman, the caravan master walk to the hole in the ground. He bent over, picking up the bucket in one hand and tossed it into the well. They watched for two heartbeats as the rope whipped through the sand, following the bucket into the hole. Suddenly the line stopped. Wyman began pulling on it, trying to recover the desert's most precious treasure, water. The bucket emerged from the well a few moments later. Wyman pulled it up by the handle.

"Hey everyone!" Wyman shouted at the top of his lungs. His face, sun-damaged from his years in the desert, finally cracked into a smile, the first smile Annah had ever seen on it. The caravan master held the bucked above the well and tipped it slightly. A stream of water poured out, falling back down into the well. "Line up! We've got water!"

Trent tried to bolt ahead and gain the front of the newly forming water line. He felt something seize his tunic and pull him back. Turning, Trent saw that Annah had grabbed his tunic above his shoulder. He tried to escape her grasp, but it might as well be made of iron.

"What? I'm losing my place in line." Trent exclaimed.

"You owe me three coins. It's payday."

"Fine, you'll get your coins. You have to wait a bit. I still need to collect a few of my winnings to pay you."

"No, you made a bet. Pay me now." Annah turned sideways and kicked out her foot, hooking Trent's leg and flipping him into the air. He felt his breath leave his lungs as he hit the sand. He tried to speak, but he didn't have enough air.

"Listen to me," Annah said, "you are starting to get a poor reputation in the caravan. We don't need to be the group with that kind of notoriety. That's how we get assigned to the worst sites. A coin or two of some little bet might not seem like a lot, but we will all be paying for your little games in the end. Be a decent person for once."

"Sorry," Trent managed to say as he sucked some air in, "I got bored."

"Don't worry, there will be plenty of excitement to keep you busy once we get a site," Eadgar said as he walked up carrying two full water skins. "Let him go. We need to water more than the object lesson right now."

Trent scrambled --- Annah released him. He picked up a dropped water skin and set off to join the growing line.

"I've got to get my water skins filled as well." She said as she turned to leave.

"No, you don't. I already sent Cook ahead with them. Stay a moment please, let's talk." Eadgar said.

Annah stopped, unsure where this was going. Eadgar clearly had something to say, and he didn't want to say it in front of Trent.

"I've been thinking." He began, "when we get back, odds are that we won't have enough coins to simply go home. There are a lot of abandoned homes in the city. Why don't we grab one and occupy it?"

Her eyes opened wide, then narrowed suspiciously. "Let's first define what you mean by 'we'," she said, stressing that definitive. "Are you talking about the whole group of us, or just you and I cuddling up in a little love nest?"

Eadgar let loose a deep laugh. "Truthfully, I never considered that as an option. Plus, I think Trent is sweet on you. I mean, it's not like you aren't beautiful and all, but well, you are kind of intense."

She looked up into his deep brown eyes. "Intense? Is that what you call women that can beat you senseless?"

Eadgar outweighed her and towered over her, yet she knew that she could outfight him. If needs be, she could kill him. His heart wasn't hard enough to be a hardened fighter. The three years she had spent in the company of northern raiders had given her that dark edge. She knew how to kill and how to stop thinking when she did it.

True to his nature, Eadgar merely offered her a kind smile. "I'm going to get us a building and turn it into our base. We won't be sharing rooms, well, unless you want to."

"Even Trent? He's kind of a snake. I'm not sure I want his eyes following me all around the house."

"So, it was better when we all shared the same cage? Really?"

She frowned, thinking hard about their desert journey. Trent had never acted up, never misbehaved. His devious nature had only become apparent after he left the cage. She didn't like people that acted like that. Somehow, she believed, there needed to be justice in the world.

But Trent hadn't interfered with her business. So far, his efforts had only resulted in the group gaining a few small advantages. The universe tracked how people treated each other. She didn't want to be near Trent when it extracted its retribution on him, but right here, right now, he was part of their group.

"Alright, I'm in. But I don't want Trent's room anywhere near mine."

"I'll move in next door if that makes you feel better." Eadgar offered, unaware of her rapidly reawakening suspicions.

"Let's see what you find, then we'll hand out rooms. For right now, let's try not to get killed in the desert."

SPLIT UP

The caravan came to a halt at the man-sized trail marker. The marker's frustum shape, like a horse-sized pyramid whose tip had been sliced off, leaned at an odd angle as it stood half-buried in the sand. A blustery wind blew across the dunes, propelling sand into their eyes. Eadgar held his hand up to shield his face.

"What's going on?" Cook asked, jogging next to him.

"Wyman is talking with another group. It looks like they are splitting off." Eadgar replied.

"Bad weather for it. If it were me, I'd wait for the next stop." Cook said.

"Not sure that's an option. If you miss your stop, your group doesn't get the next one. You wait until the end of the trail and then cut off on your own while the caravan waits a week. If you aren't back before the caravan leaves, you get left behind."

Eadgar paused to think about what would happen to a group of people left behind, with only a few days of water in their skins. He didn't like it.

"Let's not get left behind then. By the way, how far is our

marker?" Cook added.

"I think it's the next to last. That only gives us a week to search, I guess."

Cook spit toward the ground, only to watch his wad of mucus get picked up by the wind and sail away.

They waited, watching the group of men arguing with Wyman. The cavern master seemed intent on splitting them off from the leading group. Still, the treasure hunters grumbled among themselves, not willing to leave.

"It is taking them long enough. We need to get moving or pitch tents." Cook complained.

"Maybe, maybe not. Follow me." Eadgar said as he began walking toward the group. He heard them shouting at each other as they approached, struggling to be heard over the blowing wind.

"It's not fair," One of the other treasure hunters complained, "Easter told us to skip this one. That means we get the next one!"

"No, it doesn't. The rules are the rules. You skip your marker, and you get the last marker. I don't care what Easter told you," Wyman replied, a hint of annoyance creeping into his voice.

Eadgar approached the treasure hunter and put a friendly hand on his shoulder.

"Friends, why the disagreement? I know the sand is blowing, but it will pass. Can't you just stay here and wait it out?"

"Can't do that," The treasure hunter replied. "I got word that this site has already been looted. We need the next site." As if he could convince Wyman, he added, "We're the senior group."

"Not my problem, you scut. The rules are the rules."

Wyman's accent had begun to thicken as he grew angrier.

Eadgar shook his head and offered a suggestion. "Let's not bicker. Our group has one of the last markers. If you want," Eadgar nodded toward the other treasure hunter, "our group will swap you markers. That should solve both of your problems."

Wyman offered a broad smile. "Sure, but if Easter said that it's picked over, then odds are the site is picked over. Sounds like a bad trade to me."

"That's why my new friend is going to pay us a hundred coins for the favor, plus you, good Wyman, are going to give us a better position on the next caravan." Eadgar offered, the trap shutting around them.

"A hundred coins? That seems rather steep?" The treasure hunter complained, "How about fifty?"

"Seventy-five, if Wyman gives us the third marker on the next trip?"

Wyman nodded his head up and down, agreeing with almost anything to get the caravan moving again.

"Done. Fetch yer packs and top off yer water. The trail is most likely going to be visible when the sand stops blowing in your faces." He turned and began walking back toward his mule. "Get ready, everyone!" Wyman shouted to the caravan, "We're heading out in a half-hour."

Cook leaned closer to Eagar and tried to speak softly. "Are you sure about this?"

"What's not to like? We get a minimum payoff even if we find absolutely nothing, and we get the third pick for stops on the next caravan. That sounds like a good deal to me."

"If it was such a good deal, why didn't those other treasure hunters try something similar then?"

"Relax," Eagar replied, "I've got a good feeling about this. Have you ever felt that somehow fate was guiding you? Right here, right now, I can feel it leading the way."

"Sure, straight to the final black door."

DANGER BENEATH THE SAND

"More sand," Trent complained for the hundredth time since they left the caravan three days ago. The wind had calmed a small bit, transforming from a blinding sandstorm into a continuous stream of discomfort. His eyes burned where the sand had somehow wedged between his eyelid and cornea. Tears had stopped streaming down his face an hour ago, but he doubted that was a good thing.

"Hey, at least we're not getting rained on." Eadgar offered, hunting for a sliver of humor in the situation.

"I could do with a little rain, to be honest," Annah said. She stared ahead, trying to spot where Cook had gone to. A massive dune jutted out from the desert two miles east of the trail. Cook had left four hours ago to climb it, and scout out the area.

"I wish Cook would hurry up," Trent said, worry creeping into his voice.

"Me too. I'm getting sick of waiting." Annah replied, a hint of annoyance creeping into her voice.

Edgar merely shrugged and resumed walking. They could still

see the beaten trail. The group fell in behind him, following the path between hills and past skeletons of once great trees. The trail wound back and forth as it snaked through the desert, avoiding unknown obstacles but making their journey much longer with its twisted route.

"Is that Cook?" Eadgar asked, surprised to see the man standing in the middle of the trail. The man knelt on the flattened dirt, digging in the sand near the trail's edge with his bare hands.

"It looks like him," Annah said as she advanced. She called out, "Cook! What are you doing?"

"I found something," Cook yelled back as he looked back toward her, "help me dig this out."

Annah jogged beside him and saw what he was trying to free beneath the sand. Cook gripped a curved plate that was buried in the sand. He wrenched it back and forth, trying to loosen the earth's grip on whatever had caught his attention.

Annah knelt beside the plate and began to dig. Her hands stabbed into the sand, only to be met by a denser layer beneath. She brushed the sand aside to see the plate impaled into what looked like a layer of sandstone.

"Ah, that isn't good. I don't have any tools," Annah said.

Cook grunted before he replied, "Just keep pushing back and forth. Its loosening up."

She reached out and grabbed the edge of the curved surface, and began to push. The buried thing moved slightly, but it would not come free. Annah leaned into the plate, struggling with all her strength. Muscles stood up from her neck as she pushed, her arms flexing with strain. A loud grunt emerged from her throat that rapidly transformed into a scream. She pushed, shoved, forced, and struggled to find a foothold beneath the sand. She found stable footing, enough to get a grip. She pushed hard, then with all her force, she pulled in the opposite direction. The plate slipped free of the earth. Annah struggled to maintain her balance as she stepped clumsily backward, holding the plate.

"By the gods," Cook swore as he stared at what they had uncovered. It wasn't a plate; it was a scorpion's shell. The scorpion had long since left it, or this world, and that was a good thing. The scorpion shell stood taller than Cook when Annah held it up, and twice as broad. Whatever kind of scorpion this was, Annah wanted nothing to do with it.

"Easter was right. There are big scorpions out here, all right!" Eadgar called from behind them. She turned to glare at him, only to find him grinning like a madman as they had just seen the shiniest jewel in the treasure trove, "That is awesome!"

"It's awesome until we find more of them, only trying to eat us," Annah said dryly.

Silence descended on the group as they looked at the empty carapace. It wasn't difficult to imagine a scorpion that would fill that shell.

"Am I the only one thinking that we ought to go back?" Trent said.

Cook opened his mouth to reply, but no words emerged.

Annah stood upright and began to turn, scanning the close dunes rather than the faraway horizon. Suddenly, she was less concerned about the challenges that lay further away.

"I'm betting these dunes are full of scorpions." Eadgar said, the happy not still in his voice, "Let's not get off the shallow sand. I think we can make a few more hours walk that way."

"A few more hours of walking? Aren't you thinking about getting out of here?" Annah said, surprised at his blithe disregard for the hidden dangers that might even now be crawling around them.

"What? We're just getting started. Besides, Easter already told us about these things. It isn't unplanned."

"Being told is one thing," Cook said, "seeing evidence is quite another."

"Either we walk back in danger from the giant scorpions, or we keep going, in the same danger. It's all the same to me. As long as we don't get in a situation where we are dealing with more than one, I'm confident that we can handle it." Eadgar replied.

"You're confident that she can handle it," Trent said, gesturing toward Annah.

"Yes, that too," Eadgar admitted.

Annah said nothing. She unslung her pack and thrust it into Eadgar's hands. As Eadgar began to say something, Annah turned her back on him and marched forward along the trail. She pulled her knife from its scabbard and called behind her.

"I might need some brave souls to help with the fighting. If you boys see any eight-year-old girls, send them my way."

TOWER IN THE SANDS

Annah saw the tower. It jutted up against the sky, cutting the horizon line like a misshapen tooth. They had walked through the night using starlight to guide their way. The limited amount of light had been sufficient to navigate the single trail. She didn't want to see what happened when they stood still after dark, and neither did anyone else in their small group.

Now they had a tower to explore.

Details of the tower began to emerge as they closed the distance. The tower stood eight stories tall, dwarfing the group as they assembled at its foot.

Four steps of mortared stone led to a platform that stretched around the tower. Ancient carvings stood out from tan stonework, giving the viewer a hint of the magical powers used in their creation. A blackened wooden door stood taller than Eadgar. A small trail of sand led conveniently through the cracked door as if inviting them inward.

Someone had been here recently, and they hadn't even bothered to close the door after they left.

"Will you look at that," Eadgar said, taking in the tower. Small carvings of rat faces adorned the tower wall. A carved image of a rat's head jutted out of each brick. It looked like the rats were peeking into the desert from the safety of the tower. There was no hole, but from a distance, it looked like two hundred rats were struggling to escape the tower as if their very lives depended on it.

"Yes, what fun," Trent said, sarcasm dripping from his voice, "perhaps next journey we can find a place where the snakes are crawling from."

"Don't be an ass," Annah said as she strode forward. She felt tired, and the long walk hadn't improved her mood.

At least we have arrived, she thought, but where?

"That's odd," Trent remarked, gazing up at the walls, "what's with all the rats?"

"It isn't odd. The Rat God used to be a pretty popular god back in the old days." Eadgar said.

"Why is there a Rat God temple in the middle of the desert with nothing in sight?" Annah asked.

Eadgar grimaced as if a thought had made him uncomfortable. "I'm guessing when this temple was built, three wasn't a desert here. Back then, when people worshiped the First Gods, this may have been a fertile land. Now, well, it's all gone."

"But this building can't be that old. Someone built it. If your guess is right, that means that the desert has been here less than a thousand years. Is that even possible?" Annah replied, a hint of disbelief coming into her voice.

"Unless the desert is a curse," Cook said. He turned his head and spit phlegm onto the sand.

Annah grimaced, "What could curse an entire land? I've never heard of such a thing, even in the legends."

Edgar walked forward, gently laying his hand on one of the many carved rat heads that decorated the walls. "One of the First Gods could do such a thing."

Turning around, Annah gazed at the sprawling desert that

continued on into nothingness. Could one of the First Gods really do such a thing?

She didn't believe it. "Are you telling me that some god of rats cursed the entire land? A Rat God that has been gone for centuries?"

"Don't be foolish," Eadgar said, "The First Gods aren't gone. They never left this world. They are more a part of this world than you and I. People don't see much of them anymore. They have tired of us, I'm afraid."

"You think too much," Annah said as she grabbed the door, pulling it open then walking in.

Annah strode in, her heels pounding on the wooden floor, sending echoes throughout the two-story room. A narrow stair stood against the left wall. She wondered if it would collapse if she tried to climb them. Opposite the door, a multicolored mosaic covered the entire wall.

An image of an animal decorated each corner of the mosaic. The figure of a rat standing on its hind legs was painted on the lower left while a lion reared above it on the upper left corner. A bear had been beautifully rendered in black jade on the right top.

The lower right stood bare, its image pealed away long ago.

"It's a map," Cook said as he walked in behind her, "I know, it's obvious."

"Not so obvious. I think it's more than a map. Look at the corners," Eadgar said as he haled forward, holding out his hand and feeling the empty place on the lower right of the mosaic.

The image showed an outline of the lands that features broad rivers and brown roads that meandered across the image. The blue and brown trails on the tiles crossed lush green areas. Five stone carvings, each in the shape of a town or village, had been mounted atop the map. A hole lay in the center of the mosaic, bashed into its center. Chips of black, green, and yellow clay littered the floor beneath it.

Cook signed in exasperation. "Why us? It's like the world hates me."

"Yes, join the club," Trent added, "Look on the good side. We didn't get stung by giant scorpions the whole way here."

"True, but we still need to make it back," Cook said.

Eadgar's voice came from the other side of the room, "Hey Annah, take a look at this mural. Doesn't this look recent?"

Annah didn't have to approach closely to see how the damage was laid out. The gap in the mural felt like a wound on the lower right of the image. She felt empty when she looked at it as if something had been there that was very personal to her. The black and green stone chips lay scattered underfoot.

"Yes, that was recent, all right. I'll bet that happened sometime in the last month." She walked forward and bent down to inspect the wreckage. Then she walked over to the gap in the center of the mural. Running her hand along, she tried where stones should be, trying to conjure an image of what had been there before. She felt the small nubs of broken mortar and glue beneath. It had been more of the same kind of wreckage. But this cleared area looked much larger than the other.

Annah wondered aloud, "Was someone trying to keep this secret?"

"Or perhaps trying to protect the next group of people who came through," Eadgar added, unsure how to regard this sabotage.

"You think too highly of other people. When was the last time someone tried to help us?" Annah asked.

"I'm helpful," Trent supplied, flashing a grin.

"You're just hopeful, not helpful," Cook said, a smile crossing his pockmarked face. A slight blush began to spread across his face as he looked at Annah.

She began to giggle, "You two are idiots. Get upstairs and look for anything that might fetch a price. Eadgar and I will stay here and try to decipher this map."

"They both mean well," Eadgar began as Trent and Cook navigated the stairs. She watched as one of the steps came apart under Cook's weight, and his foot shot through to dangle in mid-air. He caught himself by falling on the next stair and grabbing tightly. After a few artful curse words, Cook managed to scramble up and continue his climb to the next floor.

Annah smiled back at him, laughter dancing in her eyes.

"They're both idiots," she said.

"Yes, but one can cook," Eadgar said.

"And the other one calls himself a cook, but isn't." She said, laughing at the humor of Cook's name. His father wanted him to be a cook and went so far as to name him thus. Cook couldn't boil water without burning it. Oddly, Trent turned out to be a good cook. He didn't have any training, but like many things, it seemed to come naturally to him.

"Have you thought about the house idea?" Eadgar asked.

"Sure, but I'm not ready to make a final decision. Trent has been behaving fine, and Cook had never been a problem for me. I'm leaning toward agreeing to share a house. Let's finish this treasure run first, can we?"

"What about this map?" Annah asked.

"Seems kind of obvious to me," Eadgar began as he pointed at the ruined gap in the center of the mosaic, "We should go here and look for treasure."

"I thought that you would say that. What about this part?" She pointed at the empty corner. "Don't you think that might be a problem? Someone removed it for a reason."

"Yes, but it's just a mosaic. The thing must be five hundred years old. What could threaten us after five hundred years?"

"Besides the curse of a First God?" Annah asked, raising her eyebrows.

Eadgar looked back at the map. He walked to the left side, then to the right, spending time gazing at the images of the three First Gods.

"Maybe we won't find a curse. Maybe we'll find a few lost secrets." He said.

Annah tightened her lips in a grimace, "Isn't that the same thing?"

INVISIBLE DEATH

"Nothing," Trent complained to the other three treasure hunters, "All this way, and we found absolutely nothing. This place has been picked cleaner than a beggar's dinner."

"And not long ago either," Cook added.

Eadgar walked out of the tower. He shook his head in disappointment. Annah looked up from where she sat, relaxing on the sand beneath the tower's shadow.

"Is it really that bad?" She asked Eadgar.

"There were a few coins, and some brass decorations someone had discarded onto the floor. We've got another week and a half before the caravan comes back. It looks like we have time to go exploring."

"Exploring?" Cook asked incredulously, "Where do you suggest we go exploring? On that barren desert, or the other barren desert?" He asked while gesturing into the wasteland.

Edgar grinned. He had spent an hour studying the mosaic, especially the blue stones that had been scraped from the surface of the map. There had once been water in the center of

51

this wasteland, some of it might still be here.

"I'm guessing that way," Eadgar said as he pointed out into the empty desert, "The map had a gap on it, but I found a dozen blue stones. There was water there at some point in time."

"But is it there right now?" Cook asked, disinclined to get lost in the desert without water.

"We only need to walk for two days, then we should be there. We will turn around and come back if there isn't any water. If everything goes wrong, we can force march back to the road and use the well there." Eadgar said confidently.

"What do you think, Annah?" Trent asked, trying to distract her away from wall mural she had been staring at.

"I'm not sure. Something is there. I can feel it in my gut. I'm not sure what it is."

"How about water? Could that be what you feel in your gut?" Cook asked, a hint of sarcasm in his voice.

Eadgar held his hands up in surrender, "I'm not trying to start an argument. We've got more than enough time and nothing to do with it. I'm just suggesting that as treasure hunters, we hunt a little treasure."

Cook shook his head back and forth, "I hate deviating from a plan."

"Plans are based on assumptions. When the assumptions change, we change the plan," Annah said.

Trent nodded his head up and down, "If Annah's in, I'm in."□

A DEATH WIZARD

Annah felt the sting of sand in her eyes. She rubbed it, trying to dislodge the particle that had wedged itself beneath her eyelid.

"You've got to be kidding me," She complained as she rubbed, making the sting in her eye worse.

"A little sand? Bothering you? Really?" Trent playfully teased as he walked off, trying to lead the group into the ancient graveyard, and failing. The other three stopped to talk.

"So, let's talk about the search plan," Eadgar said, gesturing toward the vast desert expanse, "Want to split up into two groups? One can check the markers and see if we find any clues, the other group gets to dig up dead people."

"I'll pass," Annah said, wrinkling her face in disgust, "I'm not desecrating any graves."

"That's what treasure hunters do, you know, treasure hunters like us," Cook said, a slight laugh in his voice.

"Either way, I'm not digging anything up. I'm going to explore that crypt before it falls apart."

Annah pointed to the center of the graveyard where a lone one-story building stood. Its roof had begun to sag as the desert sapped the last of its strength away. She could see cracks in the walls a hundred paces away.

"We'll be out here for days if we try to dig everything up. I'm with Annah, let's concentrate on the crypt," Cook said.

"It looks like Trent already started. He's got his eye on that marker over there," Eadgar said, "The one with the gold tip."

Trent hadn't waited for the group to create a plan. He simply began to walk to the most valuable looking item that he could see. She smiled at his cheekiness, and she thought he might have the right of it. They could spend hours planning, all while Trent collected the most valuable treasures all by himself.

He didn't dawdle when there was work to be done. Annah found herself surprised that she had started to think kindly about him. The journey hadn't made them close enough for Trent's wishes, but it had made then closer in any case.

"Yes, we are spending too time much planning. The water will only last a few days. Let's get to searching so we can get back to the well."

Mooterah, Master of the White Hand, watched from only fifty paces away. A magical shroud of invisibility reflected light away from him. His magic protected him from being seen. The only sign of his body was two deep footprints in the sand that didn't fill with sand when the wind blew.

He watched Trent walking through the graveyard. The death-markers seemed to fight their way from the earth, reaching for the sky. Trent moved quickly between them, ignoring the bodies and histories buried beneath. This would be a perfect place for this fool to meet his end, he thought. Mooterah knew that it would not be a question whether this man would die, nor even when. It was only a question of how. He would not allow anyone to interrupt his search. A most terrible and ancient artifact of the First Gods was most likely buried here, and no one would take that from him.

The White Hand Master held his hands outward, his left arm rotated until his extended thumb pointed down while his right thumb pointed upward. He pressed each of his fingers against the opposite, left ring finger to right pinky, and extended his right thumb upward until the glyph was complete. With just the slightest trickle of power, the magic began to activate, and the glyph freed Mooterah from the world's pull. Gravity gave up its hold on him, and he began to float upward, coming to a stop as he reached waist-height, levitating above the earth.

He checked the progress of the invader. Trent continued to walk through the forgotten graveyard, unaware of his peril. Glancing back toward the rest of the group, Mooterah saw that they had begun to split up. The treasure-hunters could cover more ground that way. He smiled as he realized that his task just became easier. The woman moved off toward a broken crypt that lay abandoned near the center of the graveyard. The large burly man began to brush off the grave markers, more intent on reading the fates of the dead than worrying about his own. The last man quickly moved through the graveyard intent on his goal, a golden tipped marker that stood alone, shining in the sunlight.

Only the large burly man had a weapon, and that but a club. That wasn't a threat to him, but he decided to kill him last if just to let him watch his friends die, a penalty for daring to defy him with such a petty tool.

Trent's voice came from over the sand, excited and loud, "Hey! I found something!"

Cursing to himself, Mooterah began to move. Chanting the silent voice, he urged the world's magic to lift him and drove him through the air to glide above the desert sand. He flew through the grave markers, dodging silently left and right as he drifted up behind the man. Mooterah had already explored the grave marker with the golden tip. It had turned out to be a sundial. It marked the hours with its shining tip but did nothing else. It seemed like the kind of thing that would mark some sort of treasure. His earlier efforts proved that to be false. Now this stranger was going to try the same search.

Trent had begun to accelerate toward the golden grave marker. He reached out to touch it as Mooterah silently and invisibly glided up behind him.

"There's something written on the marker!" Trent announced as he saw the ancient golden runs emblazoned on the stone. Mooterah grew angry. He had spent hours cleaning off that stone, attempting to discover its secrets, and now this vagabond was here trying to steal his efforts.

Trent grabbed the golden tip with both hands and began to wrench it back and forth. It did not budge, nor did it matter. Mooterah ended the spirit flow that kept him above the earth, and he dropped to the sand, directly behind Trent.

"What?" Trent asked as he began to turn. Mooterah grabbed Trent by the hair with one hand, pulling his head back as the treasure hunter began to scream. The surprise was lost, and the necromancer knew it. He drew a dark-iron blade from the scabbard at his belt. Shivers of magic flowed from the knife, running excitedly up his arm and out into the desert. Killing time had arrived.

"Watch out!" a voice called from across the sand. The large treasure hunter could feel the magical flows. He would definitely clean up the big man last.

Mooterah moved closer, so his chest pressed against Trent's back. Quick as a snake, he reached around Trent, set the curved knife to Trent's throat, and sliced. A stream of blood sprayed out, coloring the sand red with his life's fluid.

Mooterah didn't bother with Trent's body. He released him, allowing him to fall onto the desert sand. Trent began kicking as he choked on his blood. The kill hadn't been instant, nor clean. A slight stain of blood had connected with his arm. After a slight spirit channeling, the stain disappeared, and he was yet again invisible.

Mooterah spun, searching for his next victim. He saw

another of their group turn to sprint back and join them. The big man began to move his arms wildly, trying to put together a basic protection crafting. His form looked poor. His technique felt immature.

The White Hand Master dismissed him as a threat. He would be no challenge.

Just to allow the idiot spell crafter an idea of how doomed he was, Mooterah decided to make an example of the next victim. He chanted the three words of connection, joining his magical will to a part of Cook's body. He willed the spirit channel open. He felt power blossom and gasped with joy at its magical energy. Moving quickly, he attached the channel to his new victim tightly. A moment later, Mooterah pulled back on that same channel, instantly snapping back to his magical reservoir, taking the connected parts with it. The magical force cracked like a whip.

Mooterah smiled as he watched Cook's spine ripped from his back. It flew through the air only to fall halfway between Cook's expired body and Mooterah.

Eadgar screamed again, "Run! Annah, run!"

Annah didn't hesitate. She didn't know what had just killed Cook, nor did she want to find out. She sprinted as fast as she could toward the crypt. She didn't stop to artfully seek an entrance. Instead, she slammed into the door with her full force. The door cracked down the middle and gave way. She pushed hard, moving the broken pieces out of her way, then pushed past them into the crypt.

There was no coffin in the crypt. A few weapons decorated the floor where they had fallen as their leather harnesses had rotted away. Some of the spikes bent downward. Centuries of weight pulled them from their original shapes.

A simple shelf decorated the far wall. Three plates stood on it alongside a bow. Dust covered each of them. Grime had built up from centuries of forgotten days. A single item stood out. A statue of a bird perched in the center of the table.

A chill went up Annah's spine. She felt sure the bird statue was some kind of totem, probably of one of the First Gods. She wished that Eadgar was here, he would know.

She didn't have time for a history lesson. Screams came from outside the door. One of her friends may have just met whatever had killed Trent.

"Shite!" She swore as she wildly looked for a usable weapon. She reached to the floor and began to pick up whatever looked like it could be serviceable. She judged that the collection of swords, knives, and axes must be hundreds of years old, and whoever had made them wasn't as advanced as the smiths today. She tested a sword blade, and it bent easily. Discarding the sword, she moved closer to the table and its bird statue.

"Come on bird," She said as she desperately searched the floor, "I know you must be one of the First Gods. How about a little help? I need to kill whatever just murdered my friend Trent."

None of the blades would be solid enough to fight whatever was out there. It had to be magic, she thought, or a magician. These old things would be of no use.

She stepped on something and almost lost her balance. It felt thick and round, like a mace handle.

"Perfect," she whispered as she bent down to grab it. She moved her foot and pulled. The table moved. Whatever this was, it wasn't small. She dragged it out from beneath the table. A dark black handle came into view, mixing with the shadows of the crypt. Delicate silver lines had been drawn into the handle, showing a flock of birds. She wrenched the handle back and saw the glimmering steel blade, straight and untouched by corrosion.

"Yes! Thanks, bird!" she said, unaware that she wasn't merely speaking gratitude. She was making a contract.

The blade hissed free as she gave one final pull. It was gigantic, taller than she was, untouched by time. Birds had been etched into the sword, and when it caught the sunlight, their outlines stood out in stark relief, even against the shining steel surface of the blade.

A noise came from the entrance to the crypt. Annah didn't hesitate. She grabbed the blade and jammed it through the gap in the door, even before she saw who was coming. She hoped it wasn't Eadgar as she felt the blade strike meat. An intake of breath came from the outside of the crypt. She felt a weight push the blade down. Whatever she had thrust into had just fallen.

She pushed open the remains of the door. It wasn't Eadgar's body that lay impaled on the ground. Instead, it was a stranger. The man was thin, almost emaciated. A curved knife lay in the sand next to him. He wore a lightweight robe, a delicate linen scarf, and had only a single black ring for jewelry. She was liking this sword more and more and liking that ring less and less.

She stepped over the body and called out, "Eadgar! Cook!"

"Over here!" came the reply.

She moved further out of the crypt until she could see Eadgar. He knelt in the sand, holding Cook's immobile body.

"Shite." She said. Both Cook and Trent had just lost their lives for this stupid treasure hunt. Her heart ached. They might have been friends eventually. It had been so long since Annah could count on friends, and she had begun to hope for a miracle. No one survived her friendship very long. Now there was only one left.

Tears coated Eadgar's face. He rocked Cook back and forth as she approached.

"You need to let him go. It's done." She reached down to grasp is sleeve and pull his arm back.

"No. It isn't done yet. We need to bring our two friends back."

"Eadgar, we are already at the graveyard. Cook and Trent are just two more sacrifices to this place."

He couldn't process it. He continued to hold Cook for five long minutes before his tumultuous emotions calmed.

"We need to get out of here. Help me bury Eadgar and Trent. Then we can leave."

"No," Annah said, a stab of guilt cut into her as she heard

her own cold-hearted words, "After we bury our friends, we need to get the loot. Otherwise, none of this was worth anything."

"Will loot make any difference? We'll just come out to find more until we get enough to home."

"Do you really believe anyone ever gets enough to go home?" Annah replied.

BURYING THE DEAD

Eadgar swore as he used his hand to shovel the last scoop of sand over Trent's body.

"What a waste," He continued, venting his anger.

Annah frowned. She bit her lip, as if afraid to give voice to what she was about to say, "I was just starting to warm up to him."

"He wasn't that bad. In the end, he turned out alright."

She simply nodded as she stared at the mound of sand that covered his body. Both of them knew that the wind would dig Cook and Trent out of the sand in only a few days. There wasn't anywhere more permanent to bury them. The sand was everywhere.

Only the crypt could offer shelter. Annah glanced down at the bag that contained the raven idol. Somehow, she knew it would be a bad idea to inter those bodies in that place. She didn't know if this idol had any ties to the First Gods, but she wasn't going to chance their wrath by leaving dead bodies in their crypt. It would be bad enough to loot the tomb and steal their treasures.

She glanced down at the two-handed sword that lay next to her, resting in the sand. The black scabbard, aged and decorated with a dozen splits in its leather, stood out against the white sand. It seemed to demand her attention as if it knew she had stolen it, and it wasn't happy.

"I guess that's it then. Do you have any words to say?" Eadgar asked her, unsure how she would react.

"Me? I don't have anything kind to say about anyone."

Eadgar shook his head. "They aren't asking for kind words, just an honest goodbye."

Annah looked up into the sky. She blinked a few times, perhaps chasing away the hint of a tear.

"I'm not good at these kinds of things. Most of my friends, I lost this way. They don't seem to be able to last more than a few months. I swear, I think I'm cursed," She sniffed, surprised at the hurt coming through in her own voice.

"I wanted this to work. I tried to stay distant. I guess I couldn't help myself. I let myself feel for Trent and Cook. Now they're gone. Perhaps that thing that killed them was just my curse, working where I could see it."

"You saw it?" Eadgar asked, surprised.

"Not really. I just saw the killing. Let's face it. We got lucky. If I hadn't found this sword, then we would probably all be dead right now."

"I know. I just don't know how much of it was luck," Eadgar said as he stared down at the sword.

She shook her head, "It was more a curse than luck, trust me."

They both stood there, staring down at the newly dug graves in the sand. After five minutes, Annah bent over to pick up the two-handed sword.

Annah said, "Well, they're gone now. We'll morn them when we get back to town. We had better get moving. Otherwise, it will be our bones being picked over by the scorpions."

Eadgar walked back to pick up their supplies, and they

turned from the graves to leave them behind as they headed into the desert, back toward the caravan route.

REJOIN THE CARAVAN

"I think I see them," Annah said as she squinted. The sunlight hurt her eyes as she peered into the desert, trying to find any hint of life.

Eadgar didn't bother looking up. He sat on a discarded piece of timber, happily resting while keeping his rear end as far away from the sand-dwelling insects beneath.

"That's the fifth time you've seen the caravan in the last two days," He replied with a chuckle in the back of his throat, "You had better find them soon. The well won't last forever."

She nodded, agreeing with him. They could see how the water level had decreased in the three weeks since they had left the caravan.

Annah began to pace back and forth, kicking sand in the air with her violent paces. "It's got to be them. Who else is out here?"

"Someone is," Eadgar said, thinking back to what had happened just two days before. He wondered if the sand had blown off of Trent and Cook's bodies yet. He thought about what had killed them. It had been invisible when it struck. How were they supposed to defend against something like that?

"I've been thinking about what happened in the graveyard," Eadgar began. He felt unsure about how to proceed. For the past week, Annah's mood had become sharper, as if it were ready to snap into violence at any moment.

Annah paused and scowled back at him, "And?"

"Could the thing that killed Cook be an artifact of some kind? It might be an invisible blade. It could even be a curse of some kind."

"No, it wasn't. That's the only thing I'm sure of."

"Then, what was it?"

She paused before saying what she needed to say, "It was a spell crafter of some kind. I think we will need to visit Easter when we return."

"How do you know that? What did you see?"

Annah gazed off toward the caravan as it emerged from a cloud of dust in the distance, then toward the sky. Her eyes moved as searching for something that was just out of reach.

"It's just a feeling, Eadgar, just a feeling. Call it instinct."

"Are you going to pick a fight with Easter based on instinct?" He asked, surprised. "Easter has a lot of influence in the city, let alone the treasure hunters."

"I need to find out who killed Cook and Trent. So, yes, I am."

Eadgar stood up from his perch below. He watched Annah as she gazed off into the distance, her features cold and unmoving. Her only discernible motion was to run her thumb along the inlaid sword grip in her hand. Silver outlines of black crows seemed to dance within their pattern. He shuddered as a thought struck him. He knew that Annah would never sell this sword to Easter. She would pull the truth from Easter if she had to cut him in half to do so. Given this blade's previous success in the graveyard, he thought she just might do that very thing.

"I think you were right. That sure looks like our caravan. I'm going to fill up our water supplies before they get here and empty the well."

Eadgar moved back to gather the water skins. Annah stood unmoving, watching the approaching caravan, watching the sky. Annah never moved while they approached. She stood like one of the gravestones, unyielding to the sun or heat, as the caravan snaked closer and closer. A horse eventually cut out from the main body of the train and raced forward. Eadgar could see Wyman's lean form heading their way. He waved as he approached.

"Where's everyone else?" Wyman cried out as he rode up to them.

"Not good," was all Eadgar could say. There weren't as many treasure hunters in the caravan since Eadgar last saw it, driving into the distance, seeking richer targets to explore.

"Not good either. We lost two groups entirely. Four other people got eaten by the Scorpions. What happened to the other two? Cook, and what's his name?"

Annah finally moved from her stance. "Got killed by a curse," She spit out, anger pouring from her voice. She continued, "We need to get back to Tascarcoda. Easter and I need to have a long talk."

Shaking his head side to side, Wyman spit then said, "Best to leave that one alone. Easter told us not to send anyone out there. I'm guessing he may have been onto something?"

"I would say that he was right to avoid that place."

Eadgar began to speak, "We found a graveyard. There was something we couldn't see. It killed both Trent and Cook..."

"Save it," Annah interrupted, "They don't need the details."

"Right enough," Wyman agreed, "We just need the tally."

Annah pointed behind her to where the collection of looted items decorated the ground. They had laid out their prizes carefully, preparing for this very accounting. None of it seemed very good to her, nor Wyman.

"What about that pig-sticker?" Wyman asked, pointing at the night-black greatsword that she had used to kill whatever the unseen thing was. Its black handle seemed to soak in the bright desert sun, while the silver inlaid birds reflected light into the desert.

"That's not going to get sold. I'm claiming it. It already cost me two of my friends."

"Alright, there are rules for that. We'll get it sorted out when we return."

The caravan arrived. Men began to approach the well to refill their water skins,

An angry call erupted as they saw how little water remained, "Wyman! You've got to see this! The well is almost empty."

Wyman cursed, then explained, "Two of the other wells had gone completely dry. Water supplies are dangerously low. We needed water to be here."

Eadgar held up his waterskin as he offered, "I've got some here if we need to share."

Annah scowled back at him, unhappy with his offer but unwilling to call it back.

Smiling back at Eadgar, Wyman tipped his hat toward him.

"I'm glad someone in this caravan understands that hoarding water can get everyone killed. At this point, we all live or die together, and it's all about how smartly we manage the water. Now come on, fill your flasks so we can get back on the move. Let's go!"

Twenty minutes later, all that remained in the well was a soggy patch of mud at the bottom of an eight-foot deep hole.

Eadgar, who had watched the entire process, shook his head.

"Do you think it will be enough?"

"Hopefully, there is one more well on the way back. There should be water there as well."

Annah shook her head, "We can't count on it. We need to ration."

Eadgar nodded in agreement. They both looked at Wyman. He nodded as well.

Wyman dismounted from his horse and tied it to the nearest wagon. He climbed on to the wagon bed, put two fingers in his mouth, and let out a sharp whistle. Then Wyman called everyone closer and began to explain how they were going to ration water and hopefully survive the remainder of their journey.

Grumblings of discontent came from the caravan crowd when he announced that all water would be placed under guard in the lead wagon. Some of the treasure hunters had more supplies than others, and they resented having to share.

Wyman was forced to offer some outright bribery. First, he offered larger shares of profit, then he upgraded to promises of choice treasure hunting locations. Finally, the rebellious men relented and gave up the precious water.

The caravan left the well site just before dusk. Stars had begun to shine down through the crystal-clear sky. There would be more traveling at night now, and more danger from the things that hunted in the darkness.

HAUNTED

Annah sat alone in her tent. The black Raven idol she had found in the tomb lay in front of her, nestled between her crossed legs. The idol's jet-black emptiness seemed to call out to her, telling her to touch it, to stroke it, to understand it. She shook her head, trying to dismiss the lure. This thing felt cursed to her, but for some strange reason, she kept coming back to it.

Which, of course, was why she utterly believed in the curse.

She looked around the tent. A small oil fire burned atop a strip of thin metal, illuminating the canvas tent walls, and making it smell like oil at the same time. A few weeks ago, she would have never wasted expensive oil just to look at an idol in her tent. With the lack of water, they would soon experience, the expense of some burned oil seemed minor. Indeed, if things devolved as she expected they would, no one would want to carry any oil across the desert anyway.

A shadow moved in the corner of her vision. When she turned her head to look, it was gone. She returned to gazing at the idol, all thoughts of sleep lost. Eventually, just a few dozen breaths later, the shadow moved across the tent's surface again. This time she saw it clearly, even if briefly. The tent was empty except for her, the fire, and the idol. The shadow passed again, coasting across the surface of the fabric walls like a bird in flight before vanishing.

She started looking for insects. Something was making these shadows. There were no flying insects in this tent, and none passed above its small flame. Suddenly, she felt sure that the shadow had nothing to do with insects, or perhaps even the small fire's light.

Another shadow flew across the tent's surface. Before that had vanished, another appeared on the opposite wall of the tent. Annah watched in fascination as more and more shadows appeared on the surface of the tent, only to vanish as they traveled from ceiling to wall, then to the tent's corners. The shadows began to act together, dancing in a flock like a mass of birds recently chased from their home atop a great tree.

No, she thought, they flew like a flock of ravens. But the proper word for a group of ravens wasn't a flock. She searched her memories for the correct words.

A chill ran up her spine. A group of ravens would be known as an 'unkindness of ravens'. The idea that this wasn't a good sign began to dawn on her. The idol of the Raven God stared back at her, intent on its mysterious desires. Somehow this idol knew she was here, and it knew who she was. Her hand began to shake as she realized how powerful of a cursed item this must be.

An angry yell erupted from outside the tent. The raven shadows sped in different directions, disappearing and leaving her alone in the tent.

She heard Eadgar's voice outside, trying to calm someone down.

"Look, I know you're thirsty. We all are. We've got to conserve the water."

A deep rough voice responded, "Not if we don't have as many mouths to feed, like you, for instance."

Things have gotten bad a little early, she thought. Standing, she took up the black sword in both hands and walked out of the tent, ready for help Eadgar back these fools down.

She saw the dead caravan driver lying in the sand. The fire cast shadows across his body, melding with the dark river of blood that poured from his back. Five men threatened Eadgar, edging toward him with drawn blades. She blinked, surprised how the bright stars made the scene so clear.

"Don't do this," Eadgar pleaded, trying to find a peaceful solution whatever confrontation this was becoming. Annah knew that the dead body on the ground proved there would be no such thing.

Eadgar drew his belt knife, grimacing at the distasteful idea of a fight. She didn't like how this looked either. Two of the five men had curved steel swords in their hands. One of the swordsmen began moving the sword menacingly. The other two men carried short spears. They seemed nervous, yet willing to spill a little more blood.

She glanced down at the dead man. A spear wound plainly showed on his back. Perhaps the spearmen won't be so averse to murder, after all, she thought.

The final man hefted a chain flail with three heavy spiked weights at the end. He swung it back and forth slowly as if trying to tease Eadgar, playing with him moments before the five killed him.

The men weren't aware of her, but Eadgar saw her standing there with her blade. He held up the palm of his empty hand, signaling her to stand back. He continued to speak with the men, trying to use logic to talk them from their terrible path.

"Look, you don't need to do this. The caravan will need all the fighters it has if the scorpions give us trouble."

The flail wielder spat. Most of the spittle landed a pace from Eadgar, a small trail of it hung behind, then dropped to run across the man's short beard.

"Shut your face and die with a little dignity, won't you?"

One of the spearmen interrupted, "It's nothing personal, we

71

just need to conserve a little water."

The spearman's face broke out in a twisted grin, and his eyes shone with murder. Eadgar took a step back and raised his knife defensively. It would do little good against these five.

Something clicked into place within Annah's mind. Perhaps she could show these men the length of her steel. She could probably chase them away and save the caravan from this murder. Annah knew these men were right tough. The convoy would never return to the city because they had too many people drinking their limited water supplies. Someone was not going to make it back.

Without thought, without hesitation, she leaped forward and struck out with her two-handed sword. It cut through the leering spearman's neck with barely a sound. The head seemed to pause in mid-air as it separated from his neck, then fell onto the ground only to be joined a moment later by the body.

His partner spun, surprised at the blood splashing across his face. He struggled to point the spear behind him, towards where the threat seemed to be. He was right in his choice of direction, but he was too slow. Annah moved in closer, brushing aside the shaft of the spear with her blade. She smashed down with the heavy pommel, propelling the weight of the sword hilt into the spearman's skull.

A loud crashing sound burst out as the round pommel dented his head, forming a fist-sized crater in his skull. Blood began to drip from his nose and eyes as her enemy fell to the ground.

"Need to save a little water, eh?" She said, her voice low with malice.

The swordsman that stood to her left took a step back before recovering his bravery. His partner gave him a cutting look that called his manhood into question.

The flail wielding warrior didn't waste time trying to talk about their differences. Instead, he screamed a battle cry at the top of his lungs and surged forward, swinging the deadly flail. The iron balls moved with the speed of hummingbird wings in their path toward her blade. The flail reached out, seeking to wrap its chain around the long steel blade of her sword and send the metal balls crashing into her arms to break them. The flail had been built to fight against just such sword-wielding opponents as her.

Annah did not retreat or even attempt to avoid the flail's deadly entanglement. Instead, she quickly dropped her blade low, then swung up with all her might. The edge passed between the rapidly spinning balls, perfectly timed with skill and intent. The sword cut into the attacker's hand, separating it from the rest of his arm at the wrist, sending the flail spinning into the ground. The severed hand gripped the now-blood-covered handle of the flail.

She rotated slightly to continue her swing, bashing into a swordsman's curved blade. The desert-hardened metal struck the ancient artifact. The curved blade shattered into four pieces, leaving a partial blade stub behind, smaller than the length of her index finger.

The other sword cut toward her face. She pulled back more from instinct than skill. The razor-sharp blade lightly snicked across her cheek, drawing a small tear of blood.

She pressed inward toward the swordsman. His blows came on fast, raining down in rapid succession. She didn't try to match the lighter and quicker blade blow for blow. Instead, she rotated her body a tiny bit back and forth, barely catching the blade as it descended upon her. Metal rang against metal as they fought. A few moments later, the swordsman began to tire, and she knew the fight was over. Now that the attacks had slowed, she began to strike back in earnest. She didn't strive for speed. Instead, she smashed against the lighter blade with the full force of her brute strength.

She saw the handless man on the ground, desperately trying to wrap a leather cord around his bleeding stump. Two other bodies decorated the sand, blood pouring from a severed neck, and blank eyes staring up to the sky beneath their crushed skull. The swordsman with a wrecked blade had decided that fighting wasn't in his interest. He had tossed the remains of his sword aside. Now he knelt before her, surrendering.

"Hold up, let's talk," her opponent began. She knew this man wanted to live.

The fight was over. Annah didn't want any more blood on her hands. She decided these two, maybe three if the handless one survived, would get to live. She let the sword droop as she allowed her opponent to step back.

A grateful smile broke out on her opponent's face. He lowered his blade as well.

Then, without her command, without her will, she felt her body move with lightning speed. Her sword swung upward in a blur, cutting into the swordsman's gut. Before she could perceive what she had done clearly, the blade descended again, burying itself into the chest of the one-handed man. The kneeling man began to beg for his life. His voice was broken. He shouted that he had a child to raise and that he wasn't a terrible person.

She never heard a word he said. She impaled the kneeling man with her sword, sinking it through his shoulder and down into his heart.

The world slowed down. People rushed away from her, but she could see every one of them. The caravan fled from her, grabbing weapons and trying to form some kind of defense.

She saw Eadgar standing in front of her. How did he get there?

He held up his empty hands as he spoke to her, "It's all right. The fight's done. You won. It's over."

He spoke gently to her, repeating the final words again and again, "You won. It's over." It felt like he was trying to calm a wild animal. As she looked at the carnage that surrounded her, she realized that he was.

"They were going to murder us," She managed to say as she gulped air into her lungs.

Eadgar didn't come and closer, he kept his distance but continued to talk to her from her battle frenzy.

"As soon as we went to sleep, those men were going to crawl into our tents. They didn't give me any choice…"

"You've got a choice now. Put the sword away. Let's talk about it."

Suddenly the energy that had spurred her into battle deserted her. She fell onto both knees. After a moment, she laid the sword onto the sand, allowing it to soak some of the blood away.

Eadgar walked forward and knelt across from her. He looked into her eyes as if evaluating if she was still in a frenzy. He held out a hand, then covered her hand with his as he offered comfort.

"I didn't know you were a berserker," He said, "I've never met a woman that did that in battle."

Tears began to flow. She didn't know why, she simply felt empty, sad, despondent.

"I'm not a berserker. I've been in many fights. I've never lost control like this before." Her hands began to shake as she uttered those words.

"What happened then?" Eadgar asked with a gentle voice.

She looked down at the sword, at the birds etched into the handle.

Eadgar nodded. "The blade? Do you think it is cursed?"
Glancing back toward her tent, she thought about the flock of birds she had seen just before. There was a curse all right, she just wasn't sure the curse was in this blade.

AVATAR OF THE RAVEN

Ravens flew across a blood-red sky. Annah knew she was in a dream, but she didn't know how to wake up. She stood atop a bare mountain looking down into the valley below. The two-handed sword fit snugly in her grip as she searched for something she couldn't remember.

Annah's heart beat faster as she reveled in the experience. Her senses felt sharper than they ever had before. As she looked below, she spotted a field mouse scampering between bushes, seeking cover from those that hunted from above. She looked down at her arms. The sword pointed toward the sky, and the engraved birds from the handle had moved onto her arms. Jet-black images of flocking ravens decorated her skin. She could feel the motion of the birds as they traveled across her arms. Tiny pinpricks danced on her skin as the birds flew onto her torso and down to her legs.

She wanted to call out and revel in her newly discovered freedom. She took in a lung full of air and called out her challenge to the world.

Annah awoke and looked at the roof of her tent. The ever-present flock of raven images that patrolled her tent's inner surface scattered and disappeared as she called out. She heard footsteps running toward her tent. The flap tore open as she reached for her sword. She stopped when she recognized Eadgar's surprised face looking back from the tent entrance.

"Hey, a little privacy here!" She called out. The desert could be cold at night, but lately, she hadn't felt the chill. She had gotten in the habit of sleeping with only a shift on.

"Sorry, I didn't mean to catch you at an immodest moment," Eadgar joked. After two months in the cage together, and weeks in the desert, they had seen each other's body parts from every angle imaginable.

"Are you alright? I heard a yell."

"Sure. I was having a dream. Sorry, I didn't mean to alarm you."

"Must have been quite a dream," Eadgar said as he pulled the tent flap closed behind him.

Annah paused as an odd thought came to her mind, "You aren't trying to come onto me, are you?"

Eadgar blinked, surprised at the question. "Not really. Did you want me to?"

Suddenly she became uncomfortable. She liked Eadgar but didn't want to share a bed with him. That would just get complicated. Things seemed complicated enough for her already.

"Let's not go there," she responded.

"That wasn't why I was shutting the door in any case. I was hoping you would tell me where you got the new tattoos from."

She looked back at him, confused. "Tattoos?" She asked.

Eadgar pointed at her bare arm. She looked down and saw jet-black drawings of ravens, flocking as if over some carcass or prey. They mirrored the images in her dream. A profanity escaped her lips.

"Merc!"

"What?" Eadgar asked.

"Merc!"

"What does that even mean? I've never heard that word."

She looked back at him, confused. Something is wrong here, she thought as she looked at the tattoos. She glanced over to the raven-handled sword. It's pattern directly matched the new ink that decorated her arms.

Is it ink? Is it a curse?

She looked up at the tent surface. The flock of ravens had returned to their dance. The now-familiar feeling of ice pouring down her back returned.

"Eadgar, look at the tent roof. What do you see?"

He looked up for a moment, carefully studying the tent's construction.

"A tent that needs some washing. Why? What should I be seeing?"

"Oh, lots, I think. Or maybe I'm just going crazy." Annah looked deep into Eadgar's eyes. "I think I found something powerful in that ruin."

Eadgar nodded, "I've noticed you've been a little, well, different since then."

"I think I managed to get myself cursed."

"Maybe, but maybe not," He said. Eadgar sat on the ground next to Annah.

"Can I tell you a story?" He asked.

She nodded slowly. She hated to admit it, but she had developed a liking for Eadgar's stories. She had survived months in that cage with only Eadgar's stories, Trent's offensive jokes, and Cook's dry wit. She needed a little bit of that back right now, even if only to anchor her.

"A lot of people say the place that I come from is a little backward. We are so far from civilization that the village only recently started honoring the new gods."

"Really?" She asked, surprised. The only people that still worshiped the First Gods that she knew of were the wolf-men. They were insane, running through the plains in packs, eating their freshly killed prey raw.

"So as far as First Gods went, ours was pretty good. We were a fishing village, and we followed the Turtle God. My grandfather had been the last shaman our village ever had. Actually, according to him, I would have been his apprentice shaman eventually. Grandfather said I had the sense of it, even when I was very young. Insane, right?"

"And?" She said impatiently.

"And he told me talks of the First Gods. You see, my grandfather said that he had met the Turtle God, he even went swimming with him a few times. The village lived off the fish in the lakes and they got along well, until one day."

Eagar adjusted himself, pulling his feet from beneath him, stretching out.

"Alright, I'll bite. What happened?" Annah asked.

"That's the thing. Nothing happened. My grandfather told me that one morning, the Turtle God wasn't there anymore. The people of the village grew concerned after he had been gone a few weeks. Grandfather even led a group of men into other villages and wild areas, but he never found the Turtle God. When my grandfather died, he still believed the Turtle God would return. It never did."

"So, what was the point of this story then?"

"The point is," Eadgar said as he took her tattoo-covered forearm in his hands, "The First Gods do things because they want to, not because they need to explain them to anyone. You found something out there that is more than just a magical. Whatever it is, it's connected to the Raven God. You might be cursed, or you might be privileged. Either way, you need to pay attention. The First Gods are difficult to understand. They are born from the birthing of the world. They won't have a discussion with you. They won't share their plans. The Raven God, the carrier of vengeance itself, surely won't."

She shook her head, "The First Gods have been gone a long time. Why don't you stop fantasizing about being a shaman, like your grandfather, and come up with something helpful?"

Eadgar offered a patient smile back to her. He stood and

brushed the sand from the pants, then turned to open the tent flap.

"I'll stop thinking about the First Gods when you tell me where you heard the word Merc."

He walked out, leaving Annah in silence.

RETURN TO TASCARCODA

Wyman rode toward Annah as he returned from his scouting mission. The water had entirely run dry this morning. Each of the treasure hunters in the caravan received only a half cup of the precious fluid.

"I saw the city towers. I think we will make it sometime tonight," He said as he approached.

Wyman seldom spoke with her, and never about navigating the caravan.

"Good news, I guess," She replied.

"Yes, it is."

Wyman dismounted and tied his horse to the rear of a rickety cart before he walked beside her. The idea of arriving tonight gave her a little more energy to continue the march.

"Almost there?" She asked, just to make conversation.

"Yes, almost there. That's what I wanted to talk to you about, just you and me."

"You aren't going to proposition me, are you?"

"No, don't worry about that. We've got too many bodies

lying in the sand for that kind of nonsense."

She nodded. "Then what's our business?"

"It's more your business than mine. We are coming back to the city. You killed five treasure hunters. The penalty for that kind of thing is normally death."

"Are you kidding me? They were going to murder us."

"Most of them tried to give up. From what I saw, you cut 'em down sharp-like."

She shook her head in disagreement. "Those bastards were going to murder us in our sleep, and you know it."

"I know of no such thing. Just because you suspected those men doing something like that doesn't mean that the city will see things your way."

"The city? I didn't think there was any law in that city whatsoever."

"I'm not talking about a law, more of a custom. The magicians that buy the treasures we find will enforce their own rules. Sometimes I think they make them up as they go along. There isn't a book, a document, or even a song to tell us what the rules are."

"So, what are they going to do? Banish me from the city?"

Wyman shook his head, "People who break their rules tend to die from a gruesome disease soon after returning to the city. Most people who know better simply flee from the city and take their chances with the desert."

Annah took another step, then another. She looked back toward Wayman before she asked, "Are you telling me to run into the desert?"

"I would never give such advice. I'm just saying that you may want to think about your options. If you sell that sword of yours, you would probably have enough silver to make it back home."

She didn't even think about it. "Not going to happen."

"I thought you would say that. I just wanted you aware of your options before we get back."

"Maybe I'll talk to Easter. He might help."

"He's one of the better ones. Most of the rest of them are rotten to the core. If you can't convince him to back you, I'd seriously consider selling out and getting out. You are one of the lucky ones, at least you have the choice."

She nodded slowly, unconvinced.

Wyman didn't say a word as he walked back toward his horse. He untied it from the back of the cart, then rode further down the trail.

Eadgar walked toward her. "What did Wyman want to talk to you about?"

"Oh, not much. Wyman just warned me that the magicians are probably going to murder me when we get back to town."

"Why? What did you do?" Eadgar asked.

"Perhaps I broke one of their unwritten rules." She described the conversation she had just completed with Wyman.

"That sounds so stupid."

"Yes, that's why he gave me a warning."

They continued walking toward Tascarcoda. After ten minutes of silence, Eadgar finally asked, "So what are we going to do?"

"We? Are you sure that you want to get involved with this?"

"Sure? Oh yeah. I'm more than willing to fight the forces of stupidity, at least with you on my side. My collection of friends has been getting a little thin lately."

Annah reached out and squeezed Eadgar's hand before she teased, "I don't care what everyone else says, I think you're a good man."

"Seriously, we need some sort of plan before we return."

"I'm going to find Easter and try to talk him into backing me. If his fellow treasure-hunter-magicians listen to him, maybe I'll escape with just a warning. After all, those five were the aggressors, not me."

"You struck first," Eadgar replied unhelpfully.

"Yeah, I might not want to mention that."

"You might as well," Eadgar advised, "They are supposed to be magicians, right? Don't insult them. Have you thought about talking to someone else, someone who has some influence in the city?"

"Who did you have in mind?" Annah said.

"How about the Water Mother?"

"You go right to the top, don't you? Why don't we just call on Father Desert while we are at it?"

"Because Water Mother has a temple, priestesses, and a history of helping people in need. Father Desert has a history of robbing people and leaving their dead bodies for scorpion food."

"Good point." She said, "You go ahead and try Water Mother, I'll talk with Easter. Hopefully one of us will find a way out of this mess."

"Or we could just sell the sword and leave town," Eadgar said even though he knew it would never happen.

PHYLLIS

The Water Mother's temple lay sprawled in the middle of the only splash of green in the entire city. This place would be called lush no matter what city occupied it. Thick leafy trees surrounded a rectangular building. A deep blue dome topped the temple as five grand arches opened to allow visitors within. Thick patches of uncut grass struggled to reach out of the surrounding hard-packed earth, desperate to seek out a hint of moisture. The grass thickened as it neared the walls of the temple, where the sand had stolen a portion of the sparse water hidden away beneath.

Eadgar stopped to gaze around at the park-like surroundings. He hadn't seen this much green since he had been put into the cage months ago. As he looked at the short bushes that lined the surrounding stone walkways. Shaking his head, he wondered if he would ever escape Tascarcoda, ever see the open plains or the tall pines of his land again.

"Merc." He had no idea what the word meant. It seemed to be a useful curse word. Merc only had one syllable, but he could stretch it out long enough to deposit a little emotion in it. He wondered where Annah had heard it before. Tascarcoda remained a city of mysteries. Ever since Annah had come to the desert, she had become a mystery as well.

He stared across the grassy patch looking at the open temple, at the place where a goddess lived. When he first came up with the idea of speaking with her, he didn't think about it deeply. The Water Mother was a goddess. She had power and influence far beyond anyone he had ever dealt with. He had never even seen a deity in person before.

What am I doing? I'm going to get us a bad reputation with a goddess, he thought to himself. He considered simply walking away and abandoning his plan until he saw a young woman walk out of the temple from the center entryway. The first thing about her that caught her attention was the grace she moved with. Her tight dress seemed to hug her curved body as she walked, but to some kind of rhythm, like a dance. Her long blonde hair hung to each side of her head, forming a sea of perfectly arranged golden waves that cascaded downward until her elbows. The light blue dress highlighted her stunning eyes, with a blue so lite he could see them even from twenty paces away. Her heart skipped a beat once, twice, three times before he walked forward. He took in a soft breath, as if he were trying to approach an animal, perhaps a doe, and not frighten it.

He needn't have worried. The woman looked over as he approached and spoke, "Good day. My name is Phyllis. Welcome to the Water Temple. Please come inside out of the heat."

She motioned him to enter the door she had just emerged from.

"Ah, thanks," he replied. He didn't move. After a few seconds of waiting, Phyllis's eyebrows shot up quizzically.

Her voice sounded kind and full of caring as she replied, "Are you well? Do you need medical attention? If so, you've come to the right place."

"Sorry, no, sort of. I need advice really," Eadgar tried

offering a friendly smile, "Sorry, I've never spoken to a real goddess before. I'm getting a little tongue-tied."

"I'm afraid I have bad news. You still haven't spoken to a goddess. I'm just one of the priestesses here in the temple."

Eadgar covered his eyes with his hand, embarrassed at his mistake.

"I'm so sorry. I just assumed you were the Water Mother. I don't know what to say."

She laughed. The notes of her voice sounded high and made Eadgar think of birds in flight. "I'm far too young to be Water Mother. I'm sure that she will take the mistaken identity as a compliment, fear not. What help can I offer you?"

This time he didn't get his words mixed up. "I'm not sure you can. I need advice and maybe a history lesson about the First Gods. I was hoping the Water Mother could help me."

She smiled back at him. "The First Gods are long gone. I'm not sure bringing them up in conversation with one of the new gods would be wise. What brought this interest on?"

Before he could think about the wisdom of answering that question, her presence overwhelmed his caution. Words blurted out, "We may have found a cursed artifact leftover from worshipers of the Raven God."

She scowled as she looked him over, this time more deliberately. She took in his desert stained clothing, his worn boots, his blade.

"Yes, I see what you mean. That could be interesting to the Water Mother."

She turned and walked toward the temple entrance she had emerged from calling back to her, "Follow along! Let's get you in front of the Water Mother right now."

Eadgar chased after her.

"My name is Eadgar. I only arrived here a few months ago, so I'm new at this. Sorry for the confusion."

She called back as she moved through the arched entrance, "I've been here for ten years, and I still see new things. Welcome to exciting Tascarcoda."

"Exciting? It seems pretty dead to me."

Eadgar had been so focused on speaking with the priestess, he just became aware of where he walked. The light dimmed as the harsh glare of the sun was replaced by ambient light from a set of surrounding archways and doors. The Water Temple had no doors. It relied on the surrounding open arches to channel air through the rooms. A light breeze moved into the large chamber. It flowed across a pool of water so large that Eadgar estimated he could park twelve wagons in it and still have room to get his feet wet.

Eagar stopped to take in what he saw. Phyllis stopped and turned, waiting on him. He smelled the moisture in the air.

"I've been here too long. Last year I would have called this place a small pond with lovely stonework. Now that I've been here just a few months, it looks like an oasis." Eadgar said.

"Yes. I would like to say that a love for Tascarcoda will grow on you, but that would probably be a lie. Most people come here to simply loot the city, then leave. Whatever life remains in the city will be a fleeting thing at best." She frowned as if the death of this city were a sad thing. Eadgar didn't believe that. It seemed this city should have gone through whatever final door cities go through long ago.

"Doesn't anyone want to save it?"

"Sure, they try for a little while. But how can mere humans fight the desert itself?"

"I'm guessing with magic and the power of gods? That's where I would start."

She offered a sad smile as if she were teaching the young and naive about how the world worked.

"It's too late for that. The Water Mother has devoted her entire existence to bringing life back to this city. She fights hard, and she slows down its death, but it has made little difference other than to delay the inevitable. We've even had foreign wizards come here. These White Hand magicians have been here for twenty years. Their goal has always been to save the city. It is a noble cause, even if they only want to scavenge from its drying bones."

"Why is everything so doomed?"

"If we knew that, we might be in a better position to guess at a cure. Without water, and with only the blaring sun as a resource, this city and its surrounding lands will empty. Soon this will only be broken stones and mounds of sand. The only hints we have why this might be happening lay in the oldest records of this place."

"What do they say?"

"I'll give you the short version to satisfy your curiosity. We don't have many details, so I won't be able to answer questions."

"Please, tell me."

"Follow behind then. The tale won't take long." Phyllis said as she resumed her pace. She moved around the edge of the pond. A finger-high lip had been worked into the floor, indicating where the water lay. Eadgar looked to the bottom of the pool. Even in the soft light within the temple, he could see to the floor below. The small man-made pond had been dug enough so he couldn't stand in it without submerging his head, but not more than that.

"The records tell us that about two hundred years ago, Tascarcoda stood alive and prosperous on the shores of a narrow, quick-running riverbed. In the spring, rains would come to flood the plains surrounding the city, then crops would grow rich in the summer and autumn."

"Plains?" Eadgar asked, unsure if she had read the histories of the correct city.

"They are long gone now. The plains dried up and turned to sand when the river dried up. Now let me tell the story."

Phyllis approached a door set into the temple wall. She pulled it open and descended a staircase to the floor below. Small gems shone from the walls, each providing enough illumination so he could find his way down the stairs. After fifty steps, they walked out of the door into another room. The air in this room felt crisp and moist. Gems had been socketed onto the carved roof above, so they looked like misshapen stars.

She began to walk across the room, avoiding the small ponds that decorated the floor. Within a few moments, Eadgar eyes adjusted to the low light, and he was able to follow behind easily.

"The records say that the river dried because of the wrath of one of the First Gods. At least we found two scrolls indicating an atrocity had occurred. They say that a tribe of desert dwellers arrived in the city to seek help. Some sort of sickness had begun to take hold of them. The desert dwellers had been well known to the city dwellers and had traded with them for generations, moving goods between the cities and far off ports near the sea.

"It turned out that some people in the city had poisoned the water used by the tribe. When the tribe came here, the king of the city took them in. As they slept, he sent his soldiers to murder them. Not a single trader survived. The king seized the wealth within their caravan and paid his soldiers for his treacherous victory. A shaman of the Raven God arrived in the city a month later. That shaman announced that the Raven God would claim its vengeance on the city if they did not cast down that king. According to the scrolls, the population of the city, drunk on their king's victory, decided it would be a better idea to kill the shaman. A mob attacked him and murdered him in the street. It hasn't rained in Tascarcoda since."

She stopped before opening another door, reaching out to gently grip the silver door handle. Craftsmen had toiled to carve this door. Images of fish and larger sea-creatures decorated the dark blue surface.

"Are you ready to meet a goddess?"

Before he could respond, she pulled open the door and walked   in.

FROM THE GRAVE

The hot sun rose in the east, shining light across burning sands. A forest of shadows began their daily journey as they stretched outward, birthed by hundreds of grave markers that stood sentry around a now-empty crypt. A body lay discarded in the sand.

The stinking pile of meat had been here three such mornings already, its soul long gone. But this morning would be different.

Sand blew over a dead arm, leaving streaks of light brown on the dark sleeve. A leather-gloved fist jutted from the clothing, clenched in anger, it seemed to curse the world.

The fist opened slowly. After a few moments, the arm moved. Minute by minute, the dead form began to move. It rolled onto its side and coughed. A spray of dry scar tissue burst onto the sand. The body took in a breath as it began to contract into a ball. The corpse struggled to regain its grip on life as it started to scream in agony. Hours passed by as theonce-dead thing writhed back and forth, its newly recovered voice breaking, cracking with overuse. The screams became quieter, but they didn't stop.

The body suddenly stopped moving. A moment later, it rolled onto its stomach and began to crawl onto its hands and knees. It crawled to a grave marker and began to push upward, first to its knees, then on its feet.

Mooterah stood alone in the graveyard. He looked down at his chest. His shirt had been split open when the blade had cut into him, it's three-finger thick width had punctured his heart. He offered a dire smile. The woman had done a clean job of killing him. He told himself he would be kind to her when she met her end. Returning from the dead always meant pain, but a clean death typically meant a faster return.

He took in a deep breath as he looked at the desert expanse. He knew that he needed to rest and regain some of his power, but without water, that would be a slow and painful process. The crypt door stood ajar, and the interior had been emptied by treasure hunters.

They had no idea what they had found. Mooterah had searched for the remains of the Raven God Idol since he had come to Tascarcoda. Other artifacts meant nothing to him. He had chased rumors and intuition across the desert, seeking to find the source of the desert's curse. Only a few days ago, it had stood only a few paces away. He felt sure that he was closing in.

Now someone had picked up a sword and cut him down with it. Mooterah couldn't remember the last time a sword had killed him. So uninspiring, yet surprising none the less.

He wanted to find something that might teach him how to avoid death altogether. The idol of the Raven God might have such power, or at least lead him to clues. While the First Gods left long ago, their footprints remained throughout the world. The raven idol could be a link to their magic, a link to their essence that he could explore. In his wildest fantasy, he dreamt about finding the well of first magic, drinking from it, conquering it. Men and women had found a way to become gods, if only for a few centuries, but none of them could take on the power of the First Gods.

He smiled as he thought about wielding that raw magic. None could stand against him if he drank from that well.

Treasure hunters annoyed him. This woman treasure hunter especially so. He turned to begin his journey back to the city. The beautiful thing about treasure hunters was, he thought, they always returned home to sell their baubles. He knew where he could find this woman and the idol.

WATER MOTHER

Water Mother glanced up from the pool she had been gazing in. Large wrinkles drooped beneath her eyelids. She stood, revealing a short mature woman who had gone slightly to plumpness in her age. A wide grin spread across her face as she saw them.

"Do I get some company today? Who is this?" She asked, not caring what Phyllis's answer was.

Eadgar stopped in his tracks. Water Mother didn't seem like a powerful goddess, enchantress, and mistress of all life in Tascarcoda. She looked like the kind neighbor lady that fed the neighborhood children snacks. Suddenly, Eadgar's fear melted away.

"This is Eadgar. He is a treasure hunter."

Eadgar felt a small shock as he saw Water Mother's face suddenly transform from welcoming to guarded. She spat out her next words while she sat back down, returning to her pool of water, "What does it want? Better yet, tell it to go away."

Words deserted him. No sooner had he set foot in the room

than he had ruined everything. "Please," he began, "I found something out there. I need some help sorting out the history of it."

Water Mother ignored him as Eadgar babbled on, desperately trying to pique her interest. "We had four of us. We found a graveyard. Something killed two of my friends. We need to get an idea of what we found."

She looked up, pulling her eyes away from the scrying pool. "What makes you think I have any concern? Why should I care about the old bones you stripped from the city? I can offer regrets for the loss of your two companions, but they chose the risk when they decided to steal from the dead."

Eadgar began to stutter, words smashing into each other as he tried, and failed to tell a more coherent story.

Phyllis held up an open palm to stop him. She knelt on the stone floor and bowed her head toward the Water Mother, silent.

"You know I hate it when you do that." She stared angrily back for a few moments until her eyes softened, relenting. Water Mother complained before she looked up at Eadgar, "I don't know how you got her help, so I'll listen. You only get one chance to impress me."

Soft words came from Phyllis's mouth as she continued her subservient pose, "Eadgar has found something left over from the First Gods. Given where he found it, I suspect it had to do with ravens."

A word hissed from between the Water Mother's teeth. It sounded like she combined a snake's hiss and sheer hatred. "Mooterah."

"The necromancer would be interested in this story, to be sure," Phyllis said, agreeing with Water Mother's instincts. Mooterah had been digging through Tascarcoda for at least a decade, prying up every stone in his search of relics. Mooterah displayed a particular interest in remnants of the Raven God. Phyllis didn't trust Mooterah, and Water Mother despised him.

"I'm not sure who that is," Eadgar began, but Phyllis waved

her hand rapidly, motioning him to get on with his questions. Instead of directly asking questions, he thought it would be better to tell the entire story. Eadgar began with their arrival in the city, then meeting Easter, and finally, with their journey to the desert. He ended with how Cook and Trent had been killed, and how Annah seemed to change after she recovered the raven-shaped idol. Neither Water Mother nor Phyllis interrupted him a single time during his tale.

"You've got a problem, young man." Water Mother said. She turned back to her pool, then dipped her hand into it, stirring as she began to sing a tune softly so he could barely hear it.

"I know, that's why I'm here," Eadgar said.

Phyllis stood, then gently set her hand on Eadgar's shoulder.

"You should stay here, wait for Water Mother's advice. I'll go get a bottle of wine. I suspect we will need it."

As Phyllis walked from the room, Water Mother interrupted her quiet song and called to her, "Best to bring the strong wine."

Water Mother resumed her song. Her soft lyrics seemed to dance with the sound of her hand passing through the water, stirring, caressing. Eadgar found himself becoming sleepy as he lost track of time. A yawn erupted from his mouth as he wondered where Phyllis had gone to. His legs had begun to ache some time ago, now they tingled as his legs had become numb.

How long have I been standing here? Eadgar wondered. The song and the water had hypnotized him into a temporary sleep, even as he stood motionless. He shook his head and tried to chase away the impending sleep. Then he took a step toward the Water Mother, hoping to interrupt whatever magic was lulling him to unconsciousness.

Looking over Water Mother's shoulder, Eadgar could see rippled moving across the small pool. A finger-high stone edge surrounded the water, forming a pool large enough for someone to lie in, but not much more. He gazed down into the surprisingly deep pool. His eyes had adjusted to the dim light, and now he could see how far the pool reached into the ground. The crystal-clear water allowed him to see down past the height of five men before the darkness became impenetrable. Ripples moved from the Water Mother's hand across the pool's surface, only to be met by other ripples and waves. Those waves would emerge from the depths of the water, then intersect the ripples in an odd watery dance.

Suddenly, the fatigue that had settled on Eadgar sprung away. He realized what was happing around him.

I've been in a room with a goddess while she was using her powers, and I didn't even know it.

Eadgar wanted to see it, wanted to know how a goddess connected with the greater powers. He had some knowledge of magic, mostly inherited from through his mother and his Shaman grandfather, and it fascinated him. He sat next to the Water Mother, only slightly behind her so he could see the dance within the pool. More time passed. He didn't try to fight the water and fatigue. Instead, he let it overcome him. The world faded away as it became only about the Water Mother's song, and the water's dance.

He sat and watched, yet somehow, he felt the dance, experienced the yearning as the ripples and waves mixed. He was lost in the moment and unconcerned.

Then something touched his face. He blinked and shook his head. Phyllis knelt beside him, offering a wine glass in both hands. She looked at him with a wide smile. She had just kissed him on the cheek.

"Time to wake up," Phyllis said. Her voice moved over him like warm felt wrapped in kisses. Eadgar glanced up at her, unsure how he had returned to this room.

He took the offered wine. Phyllis stood and walked behind him and fetched another glass.

This time Phyllis approached Water Mother and offered her the glass. Water Mother looked up and smiled with gratitude. "Thank you, dear. You always have perfect timing."

Eadgar sipped from the glass. The wine tasted strong. Its

sharpness jolted his senses back into the world and away from the comforting place he had been. He watched as Water Mother took a small sip, eyed the glass critically, then poured half the glass into her mouth, swallowing without tasting.

"Water spirits tell me little about your idol, but I did get some information that you won't like," Water Mother said.

Eadgar felt surprised. He wondered if she had been talking to water spirits the whole time he had been here.

"Water spirits?" He asked, unsure where this was going.

Water Mother took another long pull from her glass, then handed it back to Phyllis, empty.

"There are still spirits within the world. They live in the earth, the air, the water. The spirits continue to struggle against whatever cursed this place." Her eyes looked down as she continued, "But I doubt they will ever overcome it."

Looking at the Water Mother with new-found interest, Eadgar opened his hands, inviting more. He had just seen the Water Mother talk to spirits. She worked with those same spirits as she struggled to defeat the desert's curse. He had seen a goddess in action, directly in front of him. It felt overwhelming.

Phyllis refilled the wine glass and handed it back to Water Mother before she spoke, "What did the spirits say?"

"Nothing good, like usual. The spirits tell me that a necromancer was killed in the desert," Water Mother said.

Eadgar nodded, "Yeah, that sounds about right. Whatever ambushed us in the graveyard had known some magic, that's for sure."

Water Mother looked into Eadgar's eyes for a moment. She continued, "They also tell me that the necromancer has returned from beyond the final door, and he is on his way back to the city."

"Wait, what?" Eadgar said as his eyes grew wide in surprise, "Someone came back from the dead?"

Water Mother scowled back at him, "What part of the word necromancer did you not understand? Try to keep up."

Phyllis reached out to touch Eadgar's arm just above his

elbow, "This city had been hosting a guild of necromancer's for decades. Who do you think is buying all of the treasures that you find?"

"You're telling me that we just killed one of our customers? And now they've come back from the dead?"

"It's worse than that," Water Mother replied, "Given where you were, I suspect you just killed one of the more powerful necromancers in the city. This Mooterah we were discussing, he's a real evil bastard. He's been looking for Raven God artifacts for years, and you just found one. I imagine he won't have any problem coming to collect whatever you found, then killing you afterwards."

"What if we just give the raven idol to him, maybe apologize?" Eadgar asked, a hint of fear coming into his voice.

He felt Phyllis grip his arm tighter, "I think Mooterah will kill you anyway, just to make a point of it."

Eadgar abruptly stood, "Annah is going to meet with this Easter person. He's one of the necromancers?"

Water Mother and Phyllis looked at each other for a long moment before Phyllis dropped her eyes. As she spoke, Eadgar could here emotion in her voice, "Yes, Easter is a necromancer master."

"I've got to warn Annah," he exclaimed as he stood up, then ran from the room.

Water Mother looked back at Phyllis, "Do you see what I meant? Love won't chase the necromancers away. I'm guessing your new friend is about to get ground up into meat by your new lover."

"Love always overcomes," Phyllis replied, her voice utterly sure of herself, "Easter won't hurt either of them. He isn't evil, just conflicted."

"Conflicted is what you are when you are trying to decide what you want for breakfast. We're talking about something far worse here."

Phyllis hung her head. This argument wasn't new to either of them. She whispered the same oath she had been making for three years, since Phyllis had met Easter, since she had taken him into her bed, "I can save him. Love can save him."

She had to believe in the power of love. If love could not save his soul from rotting away from within, nothing could.

SWORD OF RAVENS

Annah leaned back in her chair. She held a mug of what she affectionately called 'skunk-beer' in her right hand, and looked out onto the thing someone tried to call a market once. Now it was just a set of tarps, tree stumps, and muddy ground surrounded by ancient buildings, each of which seemed to be competing with the next to collapse first. She looked down the street, hoping that Easter would simply walk by. She didn't want to seek him out. That would look like desperation. She knew a man like Easter knew how to take advantage of desperate people.

Her two-handed sword lay in a newly purchased make-shift scabbard below the table. She kept one foot on it just to make sure no one had any funny ideas about ownership. She had gone to the treasure-buyers and made a small profit on the few baubles they had found. She hadn't sold the sword, though. The treasure-buyer had offered a small fortune for it, but she didn't want to sell, even if it meant never leaving this desert.

How quickly things change. Annah spent time looking at the

twenty people in the market, busily going from vendor to vendor, trying to find any quality food, clothing, or alcohol before it sold out. Not long ago, she had wanted to return home, to be away from this place. The trip into the desert had altered her mindset. She didn't feel so desperate to leave anymore. When she thought about it, she knew her change of attitude probably had something to do with finding the raven-blade. The ornate black handle decorated with ravens stuck out from beneath her foot.

She knew that she had something to do before she left this city. She just didn't know what it was.

A motion caught her attention. A road stood open across the marketplace. It eventually led to where Easter resided or at least conducted business. She narrowed her eyes, unsure if she saw correctly. A familiar face walked onto the street. She recognized the young man who bought treasures. She had only done business with him a few hours ago. Now he strode toward the market with three men following behind.

She grinned. The men were more than a mile away, yet she could see them. They seemed to have a purpose as they moved through the street. Whatever she had stumbled across in the desert may have dulled her hatred of the city, but it had improved her vision. She wasn't angry about that trade.

I wonder if I even get to choose what I like anymore.

A scowl appeared on her face as the group came closer. The group paused to speak among each other, then drew closer, cutting through the market crowd. After another sip of beer, she considered her options. She knew the men were here to take the raven sword. She wasn't going to let that happen, no matter the price.

The leader of the band of thugs approached. His polished silver ring glimmered in the sunlight. The group moved closer as Annah recognized their leader from her trip to the treasure buying house.

"Tegan," She said in cold greeting. She reached down to grasp the raven sword by the hilt then stood it next to her.

"Annah, right?" the apprentice replied, "This doesn't have to go poorly, you know? You can still take the coins and leave Tascarcoda. Isn't that what you want?"

After another sip of beer, she set her cup down on the table. She remembered her old life back in civilization. Visions of her past flooded her memory as the group approached. She could smell the ocean air, taste its salt on the tip of her tongue. The tall keep and its rough angled walls that guarded the coast seemed like it was still here, next to her. Memories of oared ships assaulted her. She could see them beaching on the white sand, could see ax and spear-wielding raiders leaping from the decks to take their city, rape their women, burn, and pillage. The castle had closed their gates, leaving the foot guard to defend the gates from outside.

She remembered being out there with her companions and her friends. It was only four years ago, but back then she didn't know how to kill, not really. It was different now. The battle had been gruesome. She could feel the blood spray onto her skin like the memory had been yesterday. She felt the exhilaration of the fight. She could almost smell the sweat and blood again, like the fight still churned around her.

Her memories took her to an unwelcome place in the past. She could still feel the blood on her skin.

She blinked, then moved her right hand to her face. She felt the blood dripping down her cheek. She blinked again, then shook her head to chase the visions away.

"What is going on?"

She felt confused as if life had suddenly shifted. She saw the market, but the world had changed since she had been distracted. None of the shoppers could be seen. Four bodies sprawled on the packed dirt of the market covered in blood. She saw Tegan's head. It had been sliced cleanly from his neck and had rolled against a thin twisted tree. A spray of blood covered the trail between it and the ten paces to the head's original body.

She saw the glint of silver. Tegan's ring seemed to shine in the sun, casting blame her way. She looked at her raven sword.

Blood covered its raven-etched blade.

Confused, she walked from the market. The sword felt weightless in her hand as she moved away. She didn't know what to do, but she knew she needed help. She began to head back toward her room, toward the one person she thought she could trust, Eadgar.

GRAVE ALARMS

Easter felt the brush of cold against his spine. The final black door had opened, claiming one of his apprentices. He sat at his desk for a moment, then he began his search. His apprentice Tegan wore a distinctive ring, and Easter used his magical channels to search for the magic ring tied to Tegan's soul. He found something. A single magical thread dangled free, its connection to a living person severed clean through.

The master necromancer recognized the taste within that channel. He could feel remnants of his apprentice, Tegan. Pouring a little of his magic into the channel, he tried to strengthen it, to connect back to Tegan. He found nothing. Tegan had left the world of the living.

Easter stood, pushing the chair back away from the desk. He turned to the back of the room and faced two plain wooden chests. He took a few short steps to stand in front of one, bent down, and touched his hand to its dark brown surface. An audible click sounded. The chest opened. After a few moments of rummaging, Easter pulled out a leather sack, turned, and walked back toward the desk. He opened the bag and unceremoniously poured its contents onto the flat surface. Five metallic thunks sounded as silver rings struck the wood, a few rolled a few times like poorly shaped dice.

He had personally crafted each of these rings. He always made two rings every time he took on an apprentice. He created both for the apprentice. One ring was to guide the apprentice through life, to repeatedly remind him of where their loyalties lie. The other was to guide the apprentice through death so when the final day came, they could be found and perhaps recovered. Easter grasped the left-most ring. He remembered it vividly as it had only been two years since he had crafted it for Apprentice Tegan.

"Too soon," was all Easter could manage to say. He removed his sleek leather glove and shifted the silver ring that he grasped between his thumb and index finger. After a few moments of meditation, Easter opened the channel of seeking. It didn't take long before he knew where this ring's twin was. Visions emerged that showed him a vacant market. Easter recognized it as the market only ten minutes' walk from here. He grasped the ring in his fist and stormed out of his office.

"Raise the Alarm!" Easter's voice echoed throughout the tower. He stormed down the stairs to find Gustavo struggling out of his chair while fumbling with his dagger. The confused look on Gustavo's face was all Easter needed. "Call out the guards, get the other apprentices. I need everyone in front of the tower in five minutes! Go!" Easter Commanded as he pointed toward Gustavo, then gestured to the next set of stairs. Gustavo sprinted away, traveling the stairs two or three steps at a time. His shouts filled the rooms below.

Easter turned and climbed the stairs quickly, returning to his office. He went to the undisturbed trunk, bent to touch it, and uttered three words. Binding the spoken words with a channel of intent, he opened the chest and exposed the grave. The chest's exterior looked like a worn iron-bound oak chest, strong enough to hold treasure, and secure enough to dissuade any but the most muscle-bound robbers. The interior was different. When Easter opened the chest's lid, he didn't look into a plain box. Instead, he looked into a grave. Magical enchantments linked the simple box to a gravesite. The opening showed a large cave below. More than fifty dismembered bodies lay wrapped in cloth and randomly tossed about on the cave's floor. Far across the desert, and even farther across the wild plains, local kings used the Robber's Cave as a place to send their criminals after execution. The local people believed that if anyone were to be sent to the Robber's Cave, the gods would curse their souls for the evil they had brought into the world.

The people were right. The Cave of Robbers had indeed been cursed, only it hadn't been the gods that had done so, it had been Master Easter. Easter looked down carefully and found what he needed. One of the bodies had begun to fester. Brown ooze had begun to slowly leak from between the cloth strips that covered the body. He nodded and channeled his will, pulling a single finger from the hand of the body. Easter caught up the finger in his gloved hand then slammed the chest shut. He turned toward the desk and opened another channel. A single rod, invisible just a few moments ago, faded into being. Easter bent down and snatched up the solid black arm's length shaft in his bare hand and strode from the office.

Easter dashed down the stairs, moving between the floors as if his life depended on it. He knew that his life was in no danger, but if he wanted to do something about Tegan, he knew that time was an enemy he could ill afford to challenge.

"Let's go!" Easter called out as he stepped out of the building. Eight people had gathered in the street in front of the door.

Gustavo stammered, "But we don't have everyone yet."

"No time to wait. This will have to do."

Master Easter strode away from the group. They fell in behind him. Three apprentice necromancers early in their studies, as well as four guards, trailed behind. Two were armored with thick leather covered with metal strips. One of the men shambled behind, a re-purposed enchanted guard that had once been a living man, but now was something much worse.

A few people had returned to the market by the time Easter arrived. His earlier vision had shown an empty place. Now the power of commercial greed mixed with a sense of inevitable demise had slowly brought the market back to life, if only barely. A few dead bodies would not stop the business of the day, even one that lay headless with a severed neck bleeding onto the packed dirt.

Easter walked up to the headless body, carefully avoiding the pool of blood that had formed near the severed neck. He shook his head, disappointed. Gustavo walked over to stand next to him.

"Lost a lot of blood," Gustavo said.

Easter nodded. Gustavo's ability to understand the obvious had always been his strength.

"There will be enough. Can you go through the market and buy a stone's weight of salt?" Easter asked.

Gustavo looked back at him, confused. Easter produced a silver coin from some hidden place in his robes and held it out to Gustavo. "I'm going to do a little necromancy. Get me some salt, then I'll explain."

Gustavo realized that the Master Necromancer was waiting on him. He nodded quickly and ran into the market, moving between booths and searching.

"You two," Easter said as he made eye contact with two other apprentices. He suppressed a grin as he recognized one of them holding a sword and breathing hard. The walk had taken the energy out of him. The apprentice struggled into one of the armored leather coats.

Easter continued, "Start gathering your channels. We are going to need a lot of power in a moment."

"Are we casting something?" the unarmored apprentice asked with a hint of excitement in his voice.

"No, we are not casting anything. I am going to see about

having a conversation with the recently departed. You two are going to channel power, so I don't need to use up my own."

The apprentices had been trained for this. They had practice sharing power dozens of times, yet rarely used it. Now was precisely the type of situation when that skill was critical. Easter could use his inner channels to do what he needed to do. If something went wrong, and it easily could, having the most potent spell crafter in their group without all of his power would be a bad idea.

Gustavo sprinted back to the group. He held a canvas bag, one hand grasping the top closed, the other supporting its weight from the bottom.

"Is that enough?" He asked between deep gulps of air.

Easter nodded. "Good job. Now pay attention and do what you are told. My two channels, I want you here." Easter pointed to where the apprentices should stand, "Gustavo, I want you next to me. Pour salt into my cupped hands when I tell you to. If I tell you to stop, then stop quickly. Walk next to me as I make the circle."

Gustavo moved in closer, thrilled to see the magic up close, yet terrified to be far away from the one person who could protect him from it.

"You others, your job is to keep people away. If anyone tries to interfere, incapacitate them. Don't be a moron and kill anyone. We don't need trouble with the locals, plus it won't be a good time to be killing anyone, trust me."

The four soldiers formed a barrier around the bodies, menacing anyone who walked too close. Quite contrary to Easter's plan, their vigilant stance attracted the attention of the market customers instead of dissuaded them from getting curious. Easter called out, "Don't get any ideas. It's going to be dangerous over here. If you get too close, you could get hurt, and not just by these guards."

The few people who had begun to creep closer stopped and took a few steps back.

"Master Easter, what about him?" Gustavo asked, a slight

high-pitched squeak in his voice as he pointed the thing that was once a man. It didn't react. It stood next to the body, looking down at it, uncaring.

"That won't matter. There isn't enough soul left in there to interfere," Easter replied.

"There isn't enough soul?" Gustavo asked.

"That's for your advanced lessons. Right now, pay attention, stay at my side, and keep the salt coming one pinch at a time. Ready?"

Gustavo nodded, "Ready."

Easter walked next to where the pool of blood and bent over. He removed his gloves and cast them aside before using his bare hands to scoop a double portion of bloody dirt.

"Salt," Easter commanded. Gustavo fumbled with his bag before producing a pinch of salt and sprinkling it gently onto the hand full of bloody soil.

"Salt," Easter said again, a hint of annoyance in his voice.

Gustavo scrambled to put more salt onto the bloody mess. He began moving pinch after pinch, carefully trying to add salt without spilling. Easter lost his patience and thrust his filled hands against the bag. "If you please, more salt," Easter demanded.

Gustavo panicked. He thrust his entire hand into the salt bag and pulled out a fistful. Holding his hand above Easter's bloody soil, he let it pour from his hands. Easter waited for it to lightly cover the surface of the mud, then walked off. He moved slowly, walking in a circle around Tegan's body. He stepped forward and bent down, then pushed the earth into a circle. Easter ran out of the mud before he made it a quarter way around the body. He stood, returned to the bloody mud then scooped two more handfuls. This time Gustavo felt ready. He reached in for more salt then poured it around the circle as he followed Easter. Five more scoops of mud and blood were enough to complete the circle.

"You might not want to stand too close. That salt is going to make it easy for the spirits to see you," Easter said as he pointed to Gustavo's salt and blood-covered hand. Gustavo took a step back.

Easter opened his channels. He searched for the circle of blood, using not only his eyes but his magics. He could feel it there being pulled between the thirsty earth and the even hungrier salt. He searched for Tegan's soul and did not find it. Instead, he found a trail, a marker where the final black door had so recently opened.

Easter pushed against the final black door. A gaping wound in the universe ripped open, howling as the wind rushed in. Tying his will to his channels, he called out for Tegan, commanding him to come forward. An image of Tegan emerged from the rip, smoke-like in its construction. Somehow it could speak, even with no physical body.

"Master Easter?" Tegan asked, his weak voice sounding like it came from within a metal tube, "What happened?"

"Sorry to say it, but it looks like someone cut off your head, and killed your companions. Can you tell me what happened?"

"Can I come back? It's dark over here."

Easter offered a slow nod, "Sure. It will take me a while to get things together, but you aren't that mangled. I think we can bring you back. But first, you need to tell me what happened."

Tegan's ghost seemed to lose solidity for a moment. His smoke dispersed for three heartbeats before it reformed. "We were killed by a woman treasure hunter named Annah. It happened so fast. I tried to get a sword for Master Mooterah because I knew he was interested in ravens. She was incredibly fast. We never saw it coming."

Easter narrowed his eyes and asked, "Ravens?"

"Yes, I'm sure if it. The blade had engravings shaped like ravens. The woman cut through us like lightning. Her eyes turned solid black. Something is wrong with her; you've got to be careful."

Easter felt his ears pop, and the cloud of smoke exploded. Trails of it were sucked back into the gaping maw of the final black door before it shrunk and closed, sealing the world from the land of death at least for now. Easter could feel the ruins of what was once an apprentice necromancer's soul, ripped and cut apart like so much meat.

A loud raven's cry came from above.

Easter looked up and saw ravens. They covered every tree in the market. The dark birds purchased on every wagon and booth.

Hundreds of the black-eyed predators surrounded their small group. Suddenly, Master Easter felt very small and weak as he gazed on the power of a First God.

"Everyone get out of here," Easter ordered his men.

The men seemed frozen in place. Easter pushed Gustavo with his open palm and screamed, "Run for your cursed life, you fool!"

The group bolted from the market, leaving only one of their number   behind.

CONSULTATION

The door slammed open. The slightly warped and bleached surface cracked through the center, leaving a scar in the wood from the center to the ceiling.

Eadgar jumped in surprise. Blankets flew from the bed to scatter across the floor as he dug through them, desperately trying to reach his knife. His spear stood untouched against the far corner, too long for use in these confined corners.

Annah charged into the room, covered in blood. She slammed the door behind her and pulled the bar down to secure it. It wouldn't slide into place. The metal braces didn't fit. She struggled with it, trying to bar the door.

"What are you doing?" Eadgar yelled as he saw Annah's panic.

She tried to lock the bar into place again. It would not fit.

"What's wrong with the door?"

"You broke it, that's what's wrong. Stop tearing down the inn for a moment and tell me what is going on!" Eadgar stopped shouting, then lowered his voice, "Why are you covered in blood?"

She looked back to Eadgar. He saw the tears pouring down her face, smearing blood, so her face had a dark shade of red to it. Streaks of blood and tears dripped down onto her shoulders. "I killed them. I killed all of them." Her voice erupted in a shriek as she went down onto the floor. She put her back against the door and began to rock.

Eadgar walked to the window and pushed the thick burlap curtains aside.

The streets looked calm. No one chased behind Annah.

He looked back as she sprawled onto the floor. "What happened?"

Words erupted in a jumbled mess, "I don't know. Some thugs tried to take my sword," she sucked in a deep breath before continuing, "I knew one of them. He was one of the treasure-buyers. They were going to take it. I couldn't let them."

Eadgar stared down at her. "What happened to your arms, Annah?"

She lifted her arms. Tattoos covered them, tattoos that she had never seen before. Flocks of ravens seemed to dance and fly across her skin.

It looked like the birds gazed down on the world and searched for prey. "I don't know. These just appeared. It has to be the sword! I don't understand what is happening to me. I killed four people in front of the entire market."

Eadgar gazed down at her. "Why didn't you just give them the sword? Take the coins?"

She put both hands on the sword's long handle. "They can't have it. It isn't theirs," she said, a tinge of hate filling her voice.

"We found it abandoned in the desert. It isn't yours either," Eadgar said as he tried to look into her eyes. He could feel some sort of a change in her.

Her eyes hardened as she stared back into his. "No. It's mine. It's always been mine."

Eadgar stood and took two steps backward. He could see Annah quivering with both rage and excitement. He looked down at the blade decorated with raven etchings, and then at Annah and her newly arrived raven tattoos. The solution to this puzzle seemed obvious.

He spoke, "That sword is cursed, you know that."

"It isn't cursed, it's just mine."

Shaking his head, he said, "It isn't yours. That sword is something left over from the First Gods. Look at the blade. It is made for people who used to worship the Raven God."

"So?" She said petulantly.

"So, the Raven God was the god of justice, murder, carrion, and war all rolled up together. What do you think the Sword of the Raven God would be used for? Cutting bread?"

"You just made all that up," she said as her voice deepened with suspicion, "Are you trying to take my sword?"

Eadgar took a panicked step back as his eyes widened. He felt his back touch the wall. He didn't like towering over her and perhaps looking like a threat. He sank into a squat, trying to get their eyes at the same level.

"I'm saying that the sword is cursed. It has some kind of remnant magic from the Raven God tied into it. Yesterday I would have advised you to sell the cursed thing, or at least see Easter and see if he could un-curse it or something."

"And today?" Annah asked.

"And today you killed a bunch of people and changed our options. We need to flee the city. You know it," Eadgar said.

"Flee? Where do we flee to? How do we survive the desert?"

Eadgar pointed to a small trunk standing alongside his bead. It could have been a stool, if not for the telltale sign of an iron lock midway on the chest's front side.

"I've managed to save a little. I can trade it for some food and more water skins. I've also done a little work talking to the other treasure hunters and managed to figure out where a few of the water holes are, at least the ones that the cage stopped at."

She nodded, grateful for his foresight. "I'm glad you were doing some planning. I got all wrapped up in this sword."

"I've been planning since before we arrived. I just assumed that if someone were going to put us in a cage to bring us somewhere, it would not be a place we want to be."

"Again, thank you." She said. Annah reached out to gently touch his shoulder, "You're a good man."

"You just noticed?" Eadgar asked, a small laugh hiding in his voice.

"What can I say? I wasn't paying attention."

Eadgar walked over the chest and produced a key from his pouch. He fumbled with the lock until it opened, then removed three-coin pouches, a silver-handled dagger, and strangely enough, a brooch decorated with the symbol of the Water Mother.

"Eadgar, have you become a follower?" Annah asked, surprised.

"We are going into the desert. I'll take any help I can get."

She smiled back, acknowledging the sense of it. "You spend a lot of time believing in the gods. It's going to get you killed if you don't watch it."

"You're one to talk," Eadgar responded as he pointed to the raven sword, "Gods don't need belief, but they might demand some attention now and then. This is especially true when dealing with the First Gods. Trust me, we don't want their antagonism. Let's give respect where respect is due."

She stared at the raven sword. For a moment, she couldn't turn her eyes away. Images of the blade cutting through those four people in the market flashed into her mind. She knew Eadgar was right.

"Let's get out of this city before someone else gets killed," Annah said, picking up the sword.

A shiver traveled from her hand as she touched the raven sword. The jolt traveled up to her shoulders and into her spine. Suddenly she knew someone was going to get killed today, it might be her, but she definitely wouldn't die alone.

PREPARED

The solid doors of the old building smashed open as Easter moved into the structure. He moved quickly through the main room, turned to avoid the stairway upwards, then passed through a door set at the back of the room. He continued into the kitchen area. Smells of cooking onions and meat filled the room as a cook looked up to see what was happening. Master Easter ignored him and continued through the kitchen and past another wide door. A long table took up most of this room, hiding a small staircase beyond. Easter almost sprinted to those stairs but slowed as he approached.

Panic was the last thing he needed Mooterah to see. He continued down the stairs, slowing his pace at each step.

Easter arrived at the lower floor into a dank room that smelled of mold and rot. Dozens of candles stood lit on a central table, across side tables, and three wall sconces. Each candle blazed with brilliant color, red, blue, green. None of these colors felt natural. Easter felt the hum of magical forces in the air. He took a moment to breathe in and smelled metal.

He stepped onto the stonework floor, then walked beyond the candle-laden table to the next chamber. He walked down an open stairway into another room. This room was more of a work-chamber decorated with machines, pulleys, chains, and an anvil sitting atop a stone base. Master Mooterah looked up from his work.

"I don't mean to interrupt, but something has happened," Easter began.

Mooterah nodded back, then looked down at the black iron mask he had been crafting at the anvil. Designs of circles and arcs decorated the mask, pulling in power and focusing it to be used by any potential wearer. Five runes of power stood in stark relief, bold white against a black background. Mooterah caressed it with a single finger before he responded.

"Something I should care about?" Mooterah asked, a hint of annoyance in his voice.

"If you care about the First Gods, then you might care about this."

"Go on," Mooterah urged as he walked from behind the anvil. Mooterah wore a set of dark armor. Dark plates fit together to form a barrier against even the most enchanted weapons. Runes decorated every surface, pushing away any blade that might approach. Easter felt the howling of magical channels as those runes steered power to their unknown ends. Mooterah had been busy these last few days.

"One of my apprentices appears to have gotten himself murdered in the market," Easter began, struggling to make lite of the bloody event. He continued, "I brought his spirit back and had a short chat with him. He gave me the name of the woman that killed him, and he told me a curious thing."

Mooterah's responded with a flat, uninterested voice, "Really? Which apprentice? Was it anyone I know?"

"Surely, you know all of the apprentices here in Tascarcoda. It was Tegan."

Mooterah barked a laugh in response. He continued, "I don't care what happened to Apprentice Tegan. Kill the woman, torture her, sell her for a slave. Just don't bother me. I have bigger problems to deal with."

"I haven't gotten to the interesting part yet," Easter said then paused for dramatic effect, "The woman killed him with a black sword. Tegan said it was etched with ravens."

"What?" Mooterah snapped as his body went into motion, snapping back at Easter, "You waited this long to inform me?" Mooterah became a blur as he picked up the mask he had been crafting and jammed it upon his face. The metal plates scraped against each other but didn't make a sound as he dashed from the room. He shouted back towards Easter, "Raise all the guild members, all the guards! Now is our time!"

The room felt empty all of a sudden as Easter gazed around, taking in the remains of Mooterah's work. The Master Necromancer had crafted a powerful set of enchantments on that mask, but Easter didn't have time to investigate what they might be. He turned to move up the stairs quickly and slowed as soon as his foot touched the first step. He considered what might be happening above. If that raven sword was an artifact of the First Gods, then Mooterah might not have the advantage in this battle. Additional reinforcements would certainly help Mooterah's cause. Easter doubted they would have much effect against the rage of the Raven God, especially if it had chosen someone to be its avatar. Anyone, perhaps everyone that he sent to Mooterah's aid, would most likely be killed if Mooterah faced one of the First Gods. If it wasn't the Raven God, then Easter figured that his old master would not need the help anyway as he was sure to be victorious. If it was the Raven God, Easter doubted he could make any difference.

With those thoughts in mind, Easter began his slow pace up the stairs. Easter would execute his duty to the Guild, of that, there would be no doubt. If Mooterah got killed by the Raven God, so much the better.

BATTLE FOR A DYING CITY

A group of guards stood in front of the main gates.

"Oh, Shite," Eadgar said, not believing their poor luck.

A line of eight men stood with sword and shield ready. Four crossbowmen stood behind them. Annah narrowed her eyes as she looked at them, blocking their way. The guards stood in a tight cluster before the barred wooden entryway. Tascarcoda gate guards usually prepared for threats outside of the city and tried to stop them from getting in. Annah didn't like the fact that the guards were alerted so quickly and prepared to prevent people from exiting. None of her previous forays into the desert had even been commented on by the guards. Today, something seemed different.

"Not good," she said as she considered her odds of escaping the city, "hopefully they aren't looking for us yet."

"It gets worse," Eadgar responded, "look behind us."

She turned her head. She saw Easter leading a group of armed men along the street.

"Shite."

Eadgar nodded, "I know. How are we going to get out of this one? There are twenty people to fight."

"I'm hoping they will be reasonable and just let us by. After all, we will probably die in the desert anyway."

"I love your optimism," Eadgar said, a dark laugh in his voice.

The lead gate guard drew his long sword and pointed it toward Annah.

"That's close enough." The guard barked, bringing Annah and Eadgar to a halt.

Eadgar spread his hands held wide, trying to show his friendliness. "What's the problem? We're just trying to step out of the city." The spear clutched in his right hand ruined the intended effect.

"It's not us. It's those people you need to talk to," the guard said as he motioned toward Easter's approaching group. Annah turned to see both groups, then scanned for an escape route. Squat two-story buildings stood at either side of the road. An old alley stretched off to the left. Annah could see piles of rocks that had been stacked man-high midway down the alley. That escape route had been sealed long ago.

More troubling, the group of fifteen people Easter had brought had begun to fan out, positioning themselves to block the road. She could see two of their number falling back. She noted them as possible archers, or given Easter's alliance in the city, they may even be spell casters. A singular form moved in the center of the group. A tingle of warning passed up her spine as she looked at that one man. He was fully armored, complete with a full metal helmet. Up north, it would have looked common, but here in the blistering heat of the desert, such a pile of metal armor typically resulted in a death sentence for the wearer. The warrior carried an oversized mace in one hand, as if ready to bash anyone who dared stand in his way. He moved oddly, though, like a string puppet being pulled along. Annah could almost feel dark magic emanating from him.

Easter's voice came from her right. "Ho! Treasure Hunters!"

He raised a hand in greeting, offering a reassuring smile. Annah didn't trust this at all.

"Easter! What's the meaning of this? We're trying to get out of here. We don't want any trouble." Annah called back.

Easter began to slow his walk. As Annah looked at Easter, he seemed calm, reasonable. She felt like she could talk to him. She didn't feel open to speak to the other men surrounding him. They moved forward with their hands on their weapons. The two that lagged began gesturing and whispering in some lost arcane tongue. The men began to fan out and block the entire street. The armored colossus in their midst simply followed a steady pace two steps behind Easter.

Eadgar began to speak, "Can't we just talk?" but Annah cut him off, placing her open palm on Eadgar's chest.

"Look, I understand. I truly do," Easter said, "but you've gotten yourselves into something you aren't ready for. That sword you picked up is cursed. Anywhere you go, doom will follow you. Please just give it up. Give me that cursed raven blade, and I'll make all of your problems go away. I can have you on a caravan tomorrow. You'll never have to see this place again. Just give it to me. If you keep it, the sword is only going to hurt you."

Annah glared back at him. His words sounded reasonable, but in her heart, she could feel the wrongness of it. She knew that she couldn't give up the blade, especially to someone like Easter.

"Are you alright?" Eadgar asked in a whisper, concern showing on his face.

"You mean despite the impeding fight? I'm not going to give it to him."

"I know. I could tell the second your eyes turned black," Eadgar said.

"What?"

Before she could ask more, high pitch screams came from the sky. She watched as countless black ravens nearly blotted out the sun as they descended onto rooftops, dead trees, walls, and gates. Thousands of eyes looked down at the scene. A feeling of rightness coursed through her veins.

The ravens stood atop their high perches. Annah knew they looked down in judgment.

Her words felt firm in her throat as she spoke to Easter and all of his men. "You aren't getting the raven blade. It isn't yours. It will never be yours. You know that."

Easter looked from side to side, then scanned the roofs and treetops.

"I don't expect you would reconsider?" Easter said, little hope in his voice.

"No." She responded.

Easter, a master necromancer and wizard, nodded in agreement and responded, "I'd wish you good fortune, but I see you have already embraced your doom. I only regret you didn't let me help." He turned and began walking back into Tascarcoda, motioning for the others to follow along.

Only three of his soldiers fell in behind him.

"What are you doing? Come on." Easter turned his head and asked the remaining men.

"No," the taller of Easter's guards said, "Master Mooterah told us you would abandon the order in the end. We are here for the sword, and we will not accept failure."

A crossbowman stepped up, breaking through the rank of guards in front of him. He pointed the weapon at Annah's heart, squeezed the release lever, and shot its missile. A whizzing sound came from the bolt as it passed through the air, aiming to kill Annah right in front of the gate. The deadly missile never had a chance.

Annah moved without thinking, springing to the side, and avoiding the crossbow bolt. The gate guards began to rush forward. She saw most of Easter's men surge forward as well. Of Easter, there was no sign.

"Shite! Shite! Shite!" Eadgar called in alarm. He leveled his spear at the charging line of men.

She leaped toward the line of guards, drawing the raven blade and swinging it in the same motion. She felt it cut through something, someone. She didn't stop to look. A tall guardsman thrust his sword at her chest. She cut back, slicing the iron blade in two. She reversed the motion of the sword, the swung down to sever the guard's arm at the shoulder. He looked down in horror. Annah ignored him and proceeded to bring the raven blade to the rest of the guards.

Eadgar called out a warning, "Look out!"

Turning, Annah caught a glimpse of the armored man Easter had brought with him. The man didn't look very coordinated, but he was intent on placing that mace in the center of her skull. Annah leaped forward and thrust the raven blade into his lung. She struck true. An arm's length of blade sprouted out the back of the armored man, his protection no more useful than paper.

The man kept coming. He pushed the blade farther into his chest and swung his mace town toward her face. She couldn't let go of the sword, but she needed to if she wanted to escape the terrible blow. Acting on instinct, Annah pushed forward, forcing the blade into his chest until only the hilt stopped it. He tried to turn and get a better shot at her. Now she was inside his range, and the mace became difficult to wield when the battle was so close.

She pushed the blade up and watched as it slowly cut through his body. Skin and bone split as effortlessly as if his armor were made of paper. She pushed the point through his ribcage, then felt the spray of blood as it finally exited through his shoulder. The man didn't fall.

She watched in amazement as he hefted the mace up high for yet another strike. Then she cut at his leg, slicing entirely through the knee. She jumped back as the man fell, continuing to swing his mace, even though she had left his range heartbeats before.

Acting purely on instinct, Annah dove for the ground. Searing heat passed over her back. She smelled burning sulfur and something else she couldn't identify as the flaming missile passed overhead and then smashed into the far building. The fire exploded, ripping a hole into the ancient structure and lighting it ablaze. She looked up to see one of the people Easter had brought with him. The man pointed at her with his two fingers extended. She didn't know what Easter's man was trying to do, but she knew magic when she saw it.

She sprang to her feet, launching herself up from the ground. She felt surprised for a moment as she saw herself leaping high from the earth. Then she fell upon the spell caster. The raven blade flashed, cutting through his shoulder and slicing through his rib cage before it emerged. Blood sprayed out, followed by something that might have once been a lung, now it looked like a collapsed bag of ruined flesh.

Annah looked back and forth, trying to find a way out of here. She had lost Eadgar. More than a dozen bodies lay scattered across the street, cut apart by the raven blade. She stopped caring about escape. Somehow, she realized this was never about running away. It was always about vengeance. It was always about a Raven God's vengeance.

With a scream, she surrendered to the raven blade, letting it guide her hand of death.

###

Mooterah observed the melee with amusement. Blood flew with wild abandon as the raven blade cut through Easter's golem, then through one of his lowly apprentices. The thing that was once a man could probably be salvaged, but not unless Easter returned quickly. Mooterah suspected that wasn't going to happen. Mooterah didn't think the apprentice mattered much in any case. He felt a small grin spread on his face as he approached the raven sword wielder unseen and from behind.

His magic had shielded him from sight. He could see the woman's muscles rippling with strength as she cut through her foes.

He could feel victory near at hand. With the raven blade in his possessions, he knew he would uncover the mysteries of the first gods, perhaps snatch their power and use it to fight the enemies of the White Hand. Even better, with that kind of power, he would own the order. The Order of the White Hand would be renamed to The Order of Mooterah.

Gripping his knife tightly, he brought his fist above his shoulder and prepared to thrust it into Annah's back. She stood only five paces away, silhouetted by a burning building. The air felt thick with smoke and the sounds of battle. Mooterah took a step forward, moving in for his strike.

Suddenly the cries of ravens filled the air. They called down from the trees, from the rooftops. Annah spun and looked directly at Mooterah. For a small moment, he felt a rush of fear until he remembered that his magic made him invisible. A slight smile began to form on his face. Then Annah screamed a battle cry and launched herself at him, swinging her sword down onto his outstretched hand.

The sword hit his arm with a hammer-blow. He dropped his dagger. The protective spell he had placed on his armor had held. He had felt a momentary pain, but that was all. Glancing down at the ground, he saw his dagger lying abandoned in the dirt. More disturbingly, a severed arm lay next to it, cut clean through.

Mooterah quickly tried to move his arms upward to grab his left hand with his right. He had no right hand now, at least not one connected to his body. Magical flows responded to his wound. Runes in his armor focused energies into action. He could feel burning pain where the stump was. The mage-crafted armor began to cast its power outward, re-growing and re-knitting flesh. A bloody tendril of sinew, fat, and bone began to grow out of his arm's severed stump.

He didn't have time to watch his arm regrow. Annah moved forward quickly, intent on finishing him off. Words of power escaped Mooterah's lips. Fates snapped together around his body, protecting his future from harm. The raven sword came down again, this time sliding off the magical power, cutting past as it ripped the spell to shreds.

Mooterah turned to run. Behind him, a building filled with raging flame. He sprinted toward it, hoping to move through the fire and escape out the back. Annah leaped in front of him, passing over his head and landing near the building's corner. She struck out, and the raven sword cut through the corner support beam like that eight-inch timber was paper-thin. The building began leaning toward Mooterah, then suddenly, it collapsed into burning rubble. Flaming wood mixed with aged brick, falling on the square like rage from the First Gods.

Annah began to laugh with glee. This was the rage of the First Gods, or at the very least, it was the rage of the Raven God.

The fire spread from the ruined building into the wagons and makeshift shelters that decorated the street. It only took five heartbeats before they too were aflame. Crowds began to surge forward from the center of town. Men and women came to fight the fire, bravely carrying buckets unaware of the battle they were intruding upon. A chain of treasure hunters moved forward, each passing buckets to the next trying to move water from the well fifty paces away to the fire.

Mooterah didn't hesitate when he saw his opportunity. He gathered his channels and tuned them, reshaping them to become the breakers of minds. He had crafted this spell many times and driven dozens of people mad with the slightest touch. Tonight, it would be different. Tonight, he would break everyone. He released his breaker channels into the crowd of rescuers, and they went mad. Men and women dropped their buckets and screamed as their self-control was taken from them. Their spirits died in shredded rags of souls. Now a dark force came into their body and took it for their own.

The crowd turned on Annah as one, sprinting toward her, intent on murder.

The raven blade began its bloody work. Annah swung and

swung again. Each stroke ending the life of a possessed. Cut, move, cut, she whittled their numbers to less than twenty, then in a spray of blood and fury, she cut down the last group in less time it took most people to yawn.

She saw Mooterah. His hand had somehow grown back, and he stood just a few paces outside of the square. She could hear the cries of the wounded and saw Eadgar picking up a small girl from the ground. Annah wondered if the girl still lived, then remembered that she was the one who had cut her down. Rage filled her. All of this was completely unnecessary. This city had been cursed to die generations before these people had arrived. The Raven God had decreed it, and these people tried to thwart its will. Annah would not allow it.

She sprung towards Mooterah. He moved his hands and uttered something magical. Forces pulsed around him, and the raven blade struck. This time, Mooterah's magic could not protect him. The raven blade cut into the side of his head, slicing through his cheek and cutting his ear in half. He went down on a single knee and forced more power into the armor. Dark channels opened from the core of his soul like tendrils, infecting the rune-armor and turning its spell to Mooterah's will. His face burned, then instantly became whole.

The raven sword came down again, this time severing his left leg at the knee. He felt the pain, then the burning as the limb regrew. Mooterah expected Annah to tire soon, then this battle would turn in his favor.

Annah stabbed the blade through his spine, then spun him around. The necromancer lay on the ground facing upward, facing into her eyes. She looked down at him with jet-black raven eyes. Tattoos of ravens flew in flocks across her skin. Mooterah reached in gather power and found his strength was gone. The armor tried to regrow the wound, but it seemed slower than before.

She began to swing the blade, to cut, to rage. Every blow used less than a heartbeat. Every cut went deeper and deeper, her anger became bloodier and bloodier. At the hundredth swing of the raven blade, there was little remaining that was once a necromancer. All that remained of Mooterah was small chunks of meat, broken bones, and smears of blood. She turned her attention to the crowds as they madly tried to flee. These people had dared defy the Raven God. All she felt was hate as she began walking toward the fleeing people, blood dripping from her sword.

"Annah!"

Eadgar's scream came from the crowd. He staggered as he passed through their midst, then he stopped. His eyes went wide as he gazed at Annah, the power of the Raven God still upon her.

Eadgar began speaking, unsure of what to say. "What in the…"

"You dare come here? You dare steal from the dead? In my city?" She hissed back. Her voice had changed. What was once a strong confident voice had become a whistle and a hiss.

"No, I was forced to come here," Eadgar began. His grandfather had once been a shaman of a First Gods and told Eagar tales of how they communicated. Eadgar saw that Annah had somehow connected with the Raven God, and the Raven God wasn't finished yet. "Please, look around. This place is finished. It has been dying for years. Now its death is complete. Isn't that what you wanted?" Gesturing toward the city, Eadgar continued, "Look, all of Tascarcoda is aflame. It's done. The age of men has passed in this place. It now returns to you."

Flames shot up over the city. Annah watched as the fire spread from building to building, from makeshift hovel to dry wooden shelter. She gazed at the flame as all Tascarcoda burned.

"You've had your will. Can't you let Annah leave the city? Can't you let her live?" Eadgar pleaded.

Annah gazed back at him with her jet-black eyes for a moment. Then she blinked, and her eyes returned to her natural blue color. She began to shake with fear, fatigue, and the remains of battle rage. Eadgar walked up to her and took her by the arm.

"Come on, we are leaving."

She didn't respond, simply followed him out of the city and into the desert, leaving Tascarcoda to the will of the Raven God.

ASHES

Easter looked down at the smoldering city. The flames had subsided three days ago, but it was still filled with danger. Wood continued to burn beneath fallen buildings. The air smelled poisonous as if Tascarcoda's rot had been released into the atmosphere.

Water Mother walked up behind him. She set her old withered hand on his shoulder. Phyllis followed closely behind carrying a small pack and six flasks of water.

"Do you two think you will have enough water to escape the desert?" She asked.

"I don't know," Phyllis said, "This is all I could find."

Easter pointed at the flasks, "It will be enough. I won't drink much, and Water Mother... she is the Water Mother, of course."

"Was the Water Mother," the goddess said. "Now my cause is gone. I tied myself to this city and to its water a century ago. Now time has run its course, and I am no longer needed. I won't be here much longer. I doubt I will survive a day or two."

"No." Phyllis tried to deny it, but they all knew it to be true. Human gods took on power from some kind of aspect, some symmetry to a part of the universe. No one knew precisely how it was done, but they knew what the effect was. When a god's reason for being was gone, the god quickly followed.

Easter reached out his hand to take hers. "These aren't comforting words, but this is the way the world works."

"I hate it," Phyllis said, then began to cry.

"Oh daughter," Water Mother said, "do not cry. I have always known it would end this way. I tried to keep the people alive, and to let nature have a chance to heal the desert. I'm sad that I failed, but I always knew that I would not win this battle."

She gripped Easter's hand harder. "But why can't you keep going? Find another city?"

"What can I say? Sometimes we don't get to pick our fates. Like you, I didn't get a choice on how my heart would guide me."

"Like me?"

"Like you. Did you think I hadn't noticed how tightly you gripped that man's hand?" Water Mother smiled as she gestured at Easter, "A necromancer will be a poor lover, I expect, what with all that death and stuff, soon enough he will be digging up bodies and plotting world domination."

"You don't know him. He isn't like that. Easter is a good person."

Easter looked back at the two women, priestess and one-time goddess. "I'm here, you know?"

Phyllis smiled back at him. In her heart, she knew that somehow, she could save Easter from the fate he had embraced. There had to be a force in the world that could do that. She knew what the force was. It was love.

They continued gazing at the smoldering city until Easter motioned them away. They began their long journey out of the desert and away from this cursed place.

NOTE FROM THE AUTHOR

Thanks for reading my fourth book, Avatar of the Raven God. This book would have never been written, except my wife Laurie insisted on it. She wanted a book with a strong female sword-wielding main character that isn't a victim of some terrible backstory. She essentially wanted a woman to wade through gore and blood as well as, or better than her male counterparts. I started this tale with the intention of creating a three-chapter short story. The tale grew beneath my fingers, and what emerged wasn't even close to what started with. The Raven God came to call, bringing dark fates and terrible retribution to those who did not honor it. That wasn't going to be me.

This book ended up as a novella-sized standalone prequel to *A Necromancer's Apprentice*. The astute will see a few characters within these pages that had also walked in the other books. While this story takes place three hundred years before the others, its tales of magical powers, a shadowy order of necromancers, and forces beyond their control should fit within the themes of the other books in the White Hand series.

Just a note - If you liked this book, please review it, and please tell your friends.

Best Wishes

Brian P

Brian@brianphillipswriter.com
http://whitehand.brianphillipswriter.com

ABOUT THE AUTHOR

Brian Phillips lives in Northern Virginia, writes books, plays games, and lives life to its fullest. He has been in turn a sailor, a student, a Doctor of Philosophy, an engineer, and an author. He is married to the most awesome woman in the world.

www.ingramcontent.com/pod-product-compliance
Lightning Source LLC
Chambersburg PA
CBHW021203130626
46554CB00005B/1969